M

Fortune of the

Age: 23

Vital Statistics: Doelike eyes, ivory complexion.
As fragile as a china doll—and in the family way.

Claim to Fame: Did we mention that she's English
royalty?

Romantic Prospects: Many men have pursued
her for her title, but will anybody love her for just
herself?

"My whole life I've been a good girl, following the
rules, being a proper princess. But everything
changed when I met Quinn in Horseback Hollow.
He made me realize what was really important. In
his strong cowboy arms I finally felt safe. I never
should have gone back to London. Everything went
so wrong so fast! Now Quinn is acting like he hates
me. How can I possibly tell him I'm carrying his
child?"

THE FORTUNES OF TEXAS:
Welcome to Horseback Hollow

Dear Reader,

Who doesn't love a royal romance? It's a completely nonguilty pleasure for me. I also adore a cowboy romance. So when Harlequin asked me to participate in the latest Fortunes of Texas series, I was completely delighted with the opportunity to combine these two personal favorites in the quaint town of Horseback Hollow!

Amelia Fortune Chesterfield was born into a privileged lifestyle that was regrettably centered squarely in the fishbowl of royal watchers. Quinn Drummond grew up in a one-horse town, the son of an unsuccessful rancher. Everything he has today, he has worked his well-worn boots off to achieve. The pair couldn't be more different. But toss them together thanks to Amelia's newly discovered connection to the Fortune family of Texas, shake them up with one unforgettable night together and they'll discover how perfect for each other they are—if they can just keep that fact in focus when the rest of the world seems to want to get in the way....

I hope you'll enjoy their adventure as much as I did.

Best wishes and happy reading,

Allison Leigh

Fortune's Prince

———

Allison Leigh

⟨H⟩**HARLEQUIN**®SPECIAL EDITION®

Special thanks and acknowledgment are given
to Allison Leigh for her contribution to the
Fortunes of Texas: Welcome to Horseback Hollow continuity.

Recycling programs
for this product may
not exist in your area.

ISBN-13: 978-0-373-65817-6

FORTUNE'S PRINCE

Printed in U.S.A.

www.Harlequin.com

ALLISON LEIGH

There is a saying that you can never be too rich or too thin. Allison doesn't believe that, but she does believe that you can *never* have enough books! When her stories find a way into the hearts—and bookshelves—of others, Allison says she feels she's done something right. Making her home in Arizona with her husband, she enjoys hearing from her readers at Allison@allisonleigh.com or P.O. Box 40772, Mesa, AZ 85274-0772.

For all the Fortune Women.
As always, it is an honor to be among you.

Chapter One

He stopped cold when he heard a faint rustle. The only light there was came from the moonlight sneaking through the barn door that he'd left open behind him.

Standing stock-still, Quinn Drummond listened intently, his eyes searching the black shadows around him. He'd built the barn. He knew it like the back of his hand. He knew the sounds that belonged, and the ones that didn't. Animal or human, it didn't matter. He knew.

He reached out his right hand, unerringly grabbing onto a long wooden handle. He'd prefer his shotgun, but it was up in the house. So the pitchfork would have to do.

This wasn't some damn possum rooting around.

This was some*one*. Someone hiding out in his barn.

He knew everyone who lived in his Texas hometown. Horseback Hollow was the polar opposite of a metropolis. If someone there wanted something, they'd have come to his face, not skulk around in the middle of the night inside his barn.

His hand tightened around the sturdy handle. His focus followed the rustling sound and he took a silent step closer to it. "Come on out now, because if you don't, I promise you won't like what's gonna happen."

The faint rustle became a scuffling sound, then the darkness in front of him gathered into a small form.

His wariness drained away. His tight grip relaxed. Just a kid.

He made a face and set aside the pitchfork. "What'd you do? Run away from home?" He'd tried that once, when he was seven. Hadn't gotten far. His dad had hauled him home and would have tanned his butt if his mother hadn't stepped in. "Never works, kid," he advised. "Whatever you think you're running from will always follow."

The form shuffled closer; small, booted feet sliding into the faint moonlight, barely visible below the too-long hem of baggy pants. "That's what I'm afraid of," the shadow said.

Forget wariness. The voice didn't belong to a child. It was feminine. Very British. And so damn familiar his guts twisted and his nerves frizzed like they wanted to bust out of his skin. A runaway would have been preferable to this. To *her*.

Amelia.

Her name blasted through his head, but he didn't say a word and after a moment, she took another hesitant step closer. Moonlight crept from the dark boots up baggy pants, an untucked, oversize shirt that dwarfed her delicate figure, until finally, *finally*, illuminating the long neck, the pointed chin.

The first time that he'd seen her had been six months ago on New Year's Eve, at a wedding for one of her newly discovered cousins, right there in Horseback Hollow. Her long dark hair had been twisted into a knot, reminding him vaguely of the dancers at the ballet that his mom had once dragged him and his sister to. The second time that he'd seen her months later at the end of April, had been at another wedding. Another cousin. And her hair had been tied up then, too.

But that second time, after dreaming about her since New Year's, Quinn hadn't just watched Amelia from a distance.

No.

He'd approached her. And through some miracle of fate—or so he'd thought at the time—later that night, he'd taken the pins from her hair and it had spilled down past her shoulders, gleaming and silky against her ivory skin.

He blocked off the memory. He'd had enough practice at it over the past two months that it should have been easy.

It wasn't. It was the very reason he was prowling restlessly around in the middle of the night at all when he should have been sleeping.

"What the hell'd you do to your hair?"

She made a soft sound and lifted her hand to the side of the roughly chopped short hair sticking out from her head. She'd have looked like a boy if her delicate features weren't so distinctively feminine. "It's lovely to see you, too." She moved her hand again, and it came away with the hair.

A wig. It was stupid to feel relieved, but he did.

She scrubbed the fingers of her other hand across

her scalp, and her hair, the real stuff, slid down in a coil over one shoulder, as dark as the night sky. "It's a wig," she said, stating the obvious. Her voice was unsteady. "The second one, actually. The first was blond, but there were reporters at the airport, and—" She shook her head, breaking off.

That night—the night he'd twisted his hands in her hair and thought he'd tasted perfection on her lips—she'd talked about the reporters who had dogged her family's footsteps for as long as she could remember. How she hated being in a fishbowl. How her life felt claustrophobic. How she envied his life on a ranch; the wide-open spaces, the wind at his back when he rode his horse.

Again, he pushed away the thoughts. He shoved his fingertips into the pockets of his jeans, wishing he could wipe away the memory of her silky hair sliding over his chest as they'd made love. "What are you doing here?"

"In your barn? Proving I'm better at remembering a Google Map than I thought." She let out a nervous sound that was maybe supposed to be a laugh but could have been a sob.

"Not my barn," he said tightly. *"Here."*

She took a quick, audible breath. She was young. Seven years younger than his own thirty. Practically a girl. Except she wasn't a girl. She was full-grown. Self-possessed. Aristocratic.

And now, she was hiding in his barn, stumbling around for words.

"Amelia," he prompted sharply. He couldn't pretend her unexpected appearance didn't make him tense. Any more than she could hide the fact that she was clearly nervous. The way she kept shifting from one foot to the other, almost swaying, told him that.

"Yes. Right. The, um, the last time we spoke—"

"*What* are you doing here?" He didn't want to rehash that phone conversation. It had been nearly two months ago. He didn't want to think about what had precipitated it. Didn't want to think about it and damn sure didn't want to feel anything about it. Not that conversation, or whatever was making her so skittish now.

Her lips moved again but no sound came out. She lifted her hand to the side of her head again. Swayed almost imperceptibly.

And pitched forward.

He let out an oath, his heart nearly jumping out of his chest, and barely caught her limp body before it hit the ground at his feet.

He crouched beside her, carefully holding her. He caught her chin in his hand. She felt cold. And was out cold. "Amelia!"

Dim light or not, he could see that her lashes, so dark against her pale, pale cheeks, didn't so much as flicker.

He rose, lifting her in his arms. It was easy. He routinely tossed around hay bales that weighed more than she did, and she seemed even thinner now than the night he'd replaced her fancy gown with his hands. She was neither short, nor tall. Pretty average height. But that was the only thing average about Amelia Fortune Chesterfield.

Everything else—

He shook his head, blowing out a breath and carried her out of the barn, not even bothering to pull the door closed though he'd likely come back in the morning to find that possum taking up residence there again. He aimed for his truck parked up by the house, about a hundred yards away, his stride fast and gaining speed as he went. The moonlight shone down on her, painting her face an even whiter hue, and her gleaming head bounced against his arm as he ran.

He could hardly breathe by the time he made it to his truck, and it wasn't because he was out of shape. It was because the nearest hospital was in Lubbock, a good hour away.

He could deal with a lot of minor medical emergencies.

He couldn't deal with an unconscious Amelia Fortune Chesterfield.

Adjusting his grip beneath her, he managed to get the door open with one hand and settled her on the seat.

Her head lolled limply to the side, quickly followed by her lax shoulders.

"Come on, princess," he whispered, gently situating her again, holding her up long enough to get the safety belt clipped in place. The chest strap held her back against the seat and he started to draw his hands away from her waist and her shoulders so he could close the door, but her arm shifted slightly. Then her hand. Sliding over his, lighter than a breath but still enough to make the world seem to stop spinning.

"I'm not a princess," she whispered almost inaudibly.

He exhaled roughly. She'd said the same thing *that* night, too.

Only then she'd been looking up at him through her lashes; a combination of innocence and sexiness that had gone to his head quicker than the finest whiskey.

Maybe she wasn't a princess. But she was still the youngest daughter of Lady Josephine Fortune Chesterfield and the late Sir Simon John Chesterfield. And since it had come out last year that Horseback Hollow's own resident Jeanne Marie Jones was a long-lost sister of Lady Josephine, the Chesterfield family was officially one of the town's hottest topics. Even Quinn's own sister, Jess, usually practical and definitely down-to-earth, had been struck royal-crazy. It had gotten so bad lately that he'd pretty much avoided her whenever he could, just so he wouldn't have to listen to her jabber on about the latest news from across the pond.

And for the past few months, particularly, he couldn't even visit the Superette in town to pick up his weekly milk and bread without seeing a magazine on the racks that mentioned Amelia in some way.

He took her hand and set it away from him, backing away to slam the truck door closed. He strode around the front and got in behind the wheel, not wanting to look at her, yet not being able to stop himself from doing so. The dome light shining on her face was more relentless than the moonlight, showing the dark circles under her eyes.

She looked ill.

He swiftly turned the key and started the engine. "I'm taking you to the hospital in Lubbock," he said flatly.

She shifted, her hand reaching for his arm again. Her fingertips dug into his forearm with surprising strength for someone who'd nearly face-planted in the dirt. "I don't need a hospital," she said quickly. "Please." Her voice broke.

"You need something." He shrugged off her touch and steered the truck away from the house. "And you won't find it here."

She sucked in an audible breath again and even though he knew he was in the right, he still felt like a bastard.

"You fainted. You need a doctor."

"No. I just… It's just been a long trip. I haven't eaten since, well since Heathrow, I guess."

He wasn't going to ask why. Wasn't going to let himself care. She was just another faithless woman. He'd already graduated from that school and didn't need another course. "First-class fare not up to your standards?"

She ignored his sarcasm. "I was in economy." She plucked the collar of her shirt that was mud-colored in the truck's light. "I was trying not to be noticed." She turned away, looking out the side window. "For all the good that did. I managed to lose Ophelia Malone before I left London, but there were still two more photographers to take her place the second I landed." She sighed. "I lost them in Dallas, but only because I changed my disguise and caught a bus."

He nearly choked. "You rode a bus? From Dallas to Horseback Hollow?" It had to have taken hours. On top of the flight, she'd probably been traveling for nearly twenty-four hours. "You have no business riding around on a bus!"

She didn't look at him, but even beneath the rough clothes that dwarfed her slender figure, he could tell she stiffened. "It's a perfectly convenient mode of transportation," she defended.

Sure. For people like him. He was a small-town rancher. She was *the* Amelia Fortune Chesterfield. And since the day she'd returned to England after her night dabbling with Quinn—after making him believe that she was going back to London only to attend to some royal duties and would quickly return to Horseback Hollow—she'd become one half of the engaged couple dubbed "Jamelia" by the media that dogged her steps.

Amelia Fortune Chesterfield was to marry James

Banning in the most popular royal romance since the Duke and Duchess of Cambridge. *Lord* James Banning. A viscount, whatever the hell that was. A man who was her equal in wealth and family connections. A man who was slated for an even higher title, evidently, once Amelia was his wife. Earl something of something or other.

His sister had talked about it so many times, the facts ought to be tattooed on his brain.

His fingers strangled the steering wheel. "Wedding plans becoming so taxing that you had to run away from them?" He didn't wait for an answer. "Never mind. I don't want to know." He turned through the overhead arch bearing the iron Rocking-U sign and pressed harder on the gas. The highway was still a fair piece away, but once he hit that, it'd be smooth sailing. He'd leave her in capable medical hands and wash his hands of her, once and for all.

Somewhere inside his head, laughter mocked the notion. He'd been doing that so-called washing for the past two months and hadn't gotten anywhere. There had to be something wrong with him that he couldn't just file her away as a one-night stand where she belonged and be done with it.

"*Please* don't take me to Lubbock," she said huskily. "I don't need a doctor. I just need some sleep. And some food." She reached across as if she were going to touch his arm again, but curled her fingers into a fist instead, resting it on the console between their seats. "Drop me on the side of the road if you must. I'm begging you. Please, Quinn."

He ground his molars together. Would he have had more resistance if she hadn't said his name? "I'm not gonna drop you on the side of the damn road."

He should take her to Jeanne's. Recently discovered family or not, the woman was Amelia's aunt. Jeanne would take her in. Even if it *was* the middle of the night.

He muttered an oath and pulled a U-turn there on the empty highway.

Maybe Amelia wouldn't mind Jeanne's questions, asked or unasked, but Quinn would. Particularly when he had unanswered questions of his own.

He didn't look at her. "I'll take you back to the Rocking-U. And then you can start talking."

His voice was so hard.

His face so expressionless.

Amelia wrapped her arms around herself and tried to quell her trembling. She was so, so tired.

She'd foolishly thought that once she got back to Horseback Hollow, once she saw Quinn in person, everything would be all right.

She could explain. And he would understand.

He would take her in his arms, and everything would be perfect and as wonderful as it had been the night of her cousin Toby's wedding. Quinn would know that there was only him. That there had only ever been him.

It had been the single thing keeping her going throughout the dreadful ordeal of getting to Horseback Hollow.

"You can start—" Quinn's deep voice cut through her "—with explaining why you came to the Rocking-U at all."

"I wanted to talk," she whispered.

He gave her a long look. Animosity rolled off him in waves, a stark contrast to the tender warmth he'd shown her just six weeks earlier. "Yet so far you haven't said anything new."

She wanted to wring her hands. Such a silly, naive girl to think that her presence would be enough to make up for everything she hadn't said that she should have. For everything she hadn't done that she should have.

"What did Banning do? Disagree over china patterns? So you run away again to the States to bring him to heel? Your last trip here was pretty effective. Ended up with a royal engagement the second you got back home. Or maybe you're just in the mood for one more final fling before the 'I do's' get said."

"I told you weeks ago that there's no engagement," she reminded carefully. After a week of the frantic telephone messages she'd left for him once she'd arrived in London, he'd finally returned her call. She'd tried to explain to him then about the media frenzy that had greeted her at the airport when she'd returned from Toby's wedding.

Reporters shouting their congratulations on her engagement to James. Cameras flashing in her eyes. She'd been blindsided by the unwanted attention as much as she'd been blindsided by news of an engagement she and James had discussed, but had never agreed to.

He grunted derisively. "And I don't believe you any more now than I did when you said it the first time. You came to Horseback Hollow two months ago and you had sex with the poor dumb cowboy who didn't know enough to recognize things for what they were. Your little walk on the wild side, I guess, before settling down all nice and proper with the English earl."

"James isn't an earl yet." Which was the furthest thing from what she wanted to say.

"I don't give a damn what he is or isn't." He slowed to make the turn through the iron archway, but the tires still kicked out an angry, arching spit of gravel. "He's your fiancé. That's the only thing I have to know. And as good as you were in the sack, princess, I'm not interested in a repeat performance."

She bit down on her tongue to keep from gasping and stared hard out the side window until the tears pushing behind her eyes subsided. They hadn't ever made it to a "sack," as he so crudely put it. They'd made love under the moonlight in a field of green, surrounded by trees, singing crickets and croaking frogs. She'd slept in his arms under the stars and wakened at dawn to chirping birds and his kisses.

It had been magical.

"It was six weeks ago," she whispered.

He still managed to hear. "Six. Eight. Whatever it was, it no longer matters to me. You want to screw around with a cowboy, do it on someone else's ranch."

She snapped her head around, looking at him. Even though it was dark as pitch, and the only light came from the glow of his pickup truck's instrument panel, she still knew every inch of his face. Every detail. From the dark brown hair springing thickly back from his sun-bronzed forehead to the spiky lashes surrounding his hazel eyes to his angular jaw. She knew his quiet smile. The easy way he held his tall, muscular body.

"Don't do that," she said sharply. "Don't cheapen what we had."

"What we had, prin*cess*—" he drew out the word in a mocking British accent "—was a one-night stand. And the next day, you returned to the loving arms of your intended. Poor bastard. Does he know what he's getting?" He pulled to a stop in front of a modestly sized two-storied house and turned off the engine. "Or maybe he doesn't care. Maybe he's just happy to merge one highfalutin' family with another and fidelity doesn't matter one little bit."

"He's not my fiancé!"

"And that's what you came all the way here to talk about," he said skeptically. "To claim that he's not your fiancé? While every newspaper and trashy tabloid in print, every gossipy website that exists, is dissecting the great 'Jamelia' romance. If he's not your fiancé, why the hell aren't there any quotes from you saying *that?* Everything else about the two of you has been chronicled across the world. Seems to me there have been plenty of opportunities for you to state otherwise." He stared into her face for a long moment, then shook his head and shoved open his truck door. "We had this same conversation two months ago on the phone." His voice was flat. "Should have saved yourself a ten-hour flight in coach." He slammed the door shut and started walking toward the house.

"Six weeks ago," she whispered again

But of course he didn't hear her this time.

Chapter Two

Amelia finally got out of the truck and headed slowly toward him. Quinn watched only long enough to assure himself that she wasn't going to collapse again, before he turned toward the house once more. He wanted her in his home about as much as he wanted holes drilled into his head.

It was hard enough to forget about her when she'd never stepped foot in his place. Now she was going to do just that. And his need to keep her out of his thoughts was going to become even more impossible.

He shoved open the front door and waited for her to finish crossing the gravel drive. Her dark hair gleamed in the moonlight, reminding him of the last time. Only then the long strands had been fanned out around her head, and her face bathed in ecstasy.

He clenched his teeth and looked at the scuffed toes of

his leather boots. The second she crossed the threshold, he moved away. "Close the door behind you."

His steps sounded hollow on the wood floor as he headed through the house to the kitchen at the back and he heard the soft latch of the front door closing behind him.

He slapped his palm against the wall switch, flooding the kitchen with unforgiving light, and grabbed the plastic-wrapped loaf of bread from where he'd last tossed it on the counter. He yanked open a drawer, grabbed a knife, slammed the drawer shut and yanked open the fridge. Pulled a few things out and slammed that door shut, too.

None of it helped.

She was still in his damned house.

Another woman he'd let himself believe in.

Didn't matter that he knew he was to blame for that particular situation. He'd barely known Amelia. And he'd known his ex-wife, Carrie, for years. Yet he'd made the same mistake with them both.

Trusting that he was the one.

The only one.

He carelessly swiped mayonnaise on the two slices of bread, slapped a slice of cheese on top, followed by a jumble of deli-sliced turkey.

Every cell he possessed knew the minute Amelia stepped into the kitchen behind him, though she didn't make a sound. She was as ghostly quiet as she was ghostly pale.

He dropped the other slice of bread on top of the turkey and managed not to smash it down out of sheer frustration. He tossed the knife in the sink next to his elbow and it clattered noisily.

He turned and faced her, choking down the urge to take her shoulders and urge her into a chair.

She looked worse than ill.

The shadows under her eyes were nearly purple. The oversize shirt—an uglier color than the contents of his youngest nephew's diaper the last time he'd been stuck changing it—had slipped down one of her shoulders and her collarbone stuck out too sharp against her pale skin.

It wasn't just a day of traveling—by means he damn sure knew she wasn't used to—taking its toll.

"What the hell have you done to yourself?"

Her colorless lips parted slightly. She stared up at him and her eyes—dark, dark brown and enormous in her small triangular face—shimmered wetly. "You're so angry," she whispered.

Angry didn't begin to cover it. He was pissed as hell. Frustrated beyond belief. And completely disillusioned with his judgment where women were concerned.

Especially this woman, because dammit all to hell, there was still a part of him that wanted to believe in her. Believe the things she'd said that night. Believe the things she'd made him feel that night.

And he knew better.

"I should have taken you to the hospital," he said flatly. "Have you had the flu or something?" God forbid she was suffering anything worse.

Her lashes lowered and she reached out a visibly unsteady hand for one of the wood chairs situated around his small, square table. But she only braced herself; she didn't sit. "I haven't been sick. I told you, I just need food and a little rest."

"A little?" He snorted and nudged her down onto the chair seat. A nudge is all it took, too, because her legs folded way too easily. He would have termed it collapsing, except she did even that with grace.

As soon as she was sitting, he took his hand away, curling his fingers against his palm.

Whether to squeeze away the feel of her fragile shoulder, or to hold on to it, he wasn't sure.

And that just pissed him off even more.

He grabbed the sandwich, and ignoring every bit of manners his mom had ever tried to teach him, plopped it on the bare table surface in front of her. No napkin. No plate.

If she wanted to toy around with a cowboy, she'd better learn there weren't going to be any niceties. He almost wished he chewed, because the notion of spitting tobacco juice out just then was stupidly appealing.

She, of course, not-a-princess that she was, ignored his cavalier behavior and turned her knees beneath the table, sitting with a straight back despite her obvious exhaustion. Then she picked up the sandwich with as much care as if it were crustless, cut into fancy shapes and served up on priceless silver. "Thank you," she said quietly.

He wanted to slam his head against a wall.

Every curse he knew filled his head, all of them directed right at his own miserable hide. He grimly pulled a sturdy white plate from the cupboard and set it on the table. He didn't have napkins, but he tore a paper towel off the roll, folded it in half and set it next to the plate. Then, feeling her big brown eyes following him, he grabbed a clean glass and filled it with cold tap water. She was surely used to the stuff that came in fancy tall bottles, but there was no better water around than what came from the Rocking-U well. Aside from water, he had milk and beer. He wasn't sure the milk wasn't sour by now, and she definitely wasn't the type to drink beer.

"Thank you," she said again, after taking a long sip of the water. "I don't mean to put you to any trouble."

He folded his arms across his chest and dragged his gaze away from the soft glisten of moisture lingering on her full, lower lip. "Shouldn't have gotten on the airplane, then." Much less a bus.

She looked away.

For about the tenth time since he'd found her hiding in his barn, he felt like he'd kicked a kitten. Then ground his boot heel down on top of it for good measure.

"Eat." He sounded abrupt and didn't care. "I'll get a bed ready for you."

She nodded, still not looking at him. "Thank—" Her voice broke off for a moment. "You," she finished faintly.

That politeness of hers would be the end of him.

He left the kitchen with embarrassing haste and stomped up the stairs to the room at the end of the hall. He stopped in the doorway and stared at the bed.

It was the only one in the house.

It was his.

"You're a freaking idiot," he muttered to himself as he crossed the room and yanked the white sheets that were twisted and tangled and as much off the bed as they were on into some semblance of order. He'd have changed the sheets if he owned more than one set.

Once she was gone, he'd have to burn the damn things and buy different ones. For that matter, he might as well replace the whole bed. He hadn't had a decent night's sleep since learning she'd gotten engaged to that other guy within hours of leaving his arms. He was pretty sure that sleeping was only going to get harder from here on out.

He realized he was strangling his pillow between his fists, and slapped it down on the bed.

It was summertime, so he hadn't personally been bothering with much more than a sheet, but he unearthed the quilt that his mother had made for him years earlier from where he'd hidden it away in the closet after Carrie left him, and spread it out on top of the sheets. It smelled vaguely of mothballs, but it was better than nothing.

Then he shoved the ragged paperback book he'd been reading from the top of the nightstand into the drawer, effectively removing the only personal item in sight, and left the room.

He went back downstairs.

She was still sitting at the table in his kitchen, her back straight as a ruler, her elbows nowhere near the table. She'd finished the sandwich, though, and was folding the paper towel into intricate shapes. Not for the first time, he eyed her slender fingers, bare of rings, and reminded himself that the absence of a diamond ring didn't mean anything.

When she heard him, she stood. "I should go to Aunt Jeanne's."

"Yes." He wasn't going to lie. She'd already done enough of that for them both. "But it's after midnight. No point in ruining someone else's night's sleep, too. And since Horseback Hollow isn't blessed with any motels, much less an establishment up to your standards," he added even though she was too cultured to say so, "you're stuck with what I have." He eyed her. "Bedroom's upstairs. Do you have enough stuffing left in you to make it up them, or do I need to put you over my shoulder?"

Her ghostly pale face took on a little color at that. "I'm not a sack of feed," she said, almost crisply, and headed past him through the doorway.

His house wasn't large. The staircase was right there to the left of the front door and his grandmother's piano. She headed straight to it, closed her slender fingers over the wood banister and started up. The ugly shirt she wore hung over her hips, midway down the thighs of her baggy jeans.

He still had to look away from the sway of her hips as she took the steps. "Room's at the end of the hall," he said after her. "Bathroom's next to it."

Manners might have had him escorting her up there.

Self-preservation kept him standing right where he was.

"Yell if you need something," he added gruffly.

She stopped, nearly at the top of the stairs, and looked back at him. Her hair slid over her shoulder.

Purple shadows, ghostly pale and badly fitting clothes or not, she was still the most beautiful thing he'd ever seen and looking at her was a physical pain.

"I need you not to hate me," she said softly.

His jaw tightened right along with the band across his chest that made it hard to breathe. "I don't hate you, Amelia."

Her huge eyes stared at him. They were haunting, those eyes.

"I don't feel anything," he finished.

It was the biggest lie he'd ever told in his life.

Amelia's knees wobbled and she tightened her grip on the smooth, warm wooden banister. Quinn could say what he wanted, but the expression on his face told another story.

And she had only herself to blame.

No words came to mind that were appropriate for the situation. Even if there *were* words, she wasn't sure her tight throat would have allowed her to voice them. So she just gave him an awkward nod and headed up the remaining stairs. Because what else was there to do but go forward?

There was no going back.

He'd made that painfully clear more than once and her coming to Horseback Hollow to see him face-to-face hadn't changed a single thing.

At the landing, the room he spoke of was obvious. Straight at the end of the hall.

The door was open and through it she could see the foot of a quilt-covered bed.

She pushed back her shoulders despite her weariness, and headed toward it. If she weren't feeling devastated to her core, she would have gobbled up every detail of his home as she walked along the wooden-floored hallway. Would have struggled not to let her intense curiosity where he was concerned overtake her. Would have wondered how each nook and cranny reflected Quinn. The man she'd fallen head over heels in love with on the foolish basis of a few dances at a wedding reception.

And a night of lovemaking after.

The thought was unbearable and she pushed it away. She'd deal with that later.

She stopped at the bathroom briefly and shuddered over her pallid reflection in the oval mirror that hung over a classic pedestal sink when she washed her hands. It was no wonder he'd stared at her with such horror.

She looked hideous.

Not at all the way she'd looked the night he'd stopped next to her at Toby's wedding reception, smiled quietly and asked if she cared to dance. She'd looked as good that day as her gawky self was capable of looking.

But when Quinn took her in his arms and slowly circled around the outdoor dance floor with her to the croon of Etta James, for the first time, she'd felt beautiful. All because of the way he'd looked at her.

Tears burned behind her eyes again and she quickly left the bathroom behind, hurrying the remaining few feet into the bedroom. She shut the door soundlessly, leaned back against it and slid down it until her bottom hit the floor.

Then she drew up her knees and pressed her forehead to them.

He believed their lovemaking had been some sort of last fling for her, before settling down with Jimmy, whom she'd been seeing during the months before she'd spontaneously attended Toby's wedding. Quinn had accused her of that during that dreadful phone conversation. In the weeks since, he'd obviously not changed his opinion.

So how was she ever going to be able to tell him that she was pregnant?

With *his* child?

If he accused her of lying about that, too, she wasn't sure she could survive it.

She sat there, her sorrow too deep for tears, until her bottom felt numb. Then feeling ancient, she shifted onto her knees and pushed herself to her aching feet. The boots she'd borrowed from Molly, one of her mother's junior secretaries whom Amelia trusted, were too wide and too short. They, along with the ill-fitting jeans and the shirt, belonged to Molly's teenage brother as had the other set of clothes she'd started out in. They'd been left, shoved deep in the rubbish, at the airport in Dallas alongside the blond wig and the knapsack in which she'd carried their replacements.

She dragged her passport out of the back pocket and set it on the rustic wooden nightstand. Even though Molly had helped with the disguises, neither one of them had been able to think of a way around traveling under Amelia's own name. Not with security standards being what they were. All she'd come with had been the passport, her credit card and a small wad of American currency tucked among the well-stamped pages of her passport. Molly had insisted on the credit card, though Amelia had wanted to leave it behind. She knew cash was untraceable, while a credit card wasn't, and she'd stuck to it. The only thing she'd purchased had been the bus fare from Dallas. Once she'd reached Lubbock, she'd hitched a ride with a trucker as far as the outskirts of Horseback Hollow. Then, using the directions she'd memorized from Molly, she'd walked the rest of the way to what she'd hoped was Quinn's ranch. But in her exhaustion and the darkness she hadn't been certain. So she'd hidden in the barn, intending to rest until daylight.

Her head swam dizzily and she quickly sat at the foot of the bed, the mattress springs giving the faintest of creaks. She closed her eyes, breathing evenly. She didn't know whether to blame the light-headedness on pregnancy or exhaustion. Aside from her missed period, she hadn't experienced any other signs that she was carrying a baby. And if it hadn't been for Molly who'd suggested that her irregularity might *not* be a result of stress as Amelia had believed at first, she probably wouldn't know even now that she was carrying Quinn's baby. She'd still be thinking she was just stressed over the whole engagement fiasco.

Why, oh, why hadn't she spoken up when those reporters greeted her at the airport six weeks ago, clamoring for details about her engagement to James? Why had she just put up her hand to shield her face and raced alongside her driver until reaching the relative sanctuary of the Town Car? She hadn't even dared to phone James until she'd gotten home because she feared having her cell phone hacked again. Even though it had happened well over a year ago, the sense of invasion still lived on.

If she'd only have spoken up, denied the engagement to the press right then and there, she wouldn't be in this situation now. After the initial embarrassment, James's situation with his family would have ironed itself out in time.

Most important, though, Quinn wouldn't have any reason to hate her.

She would have returned to him weeks ago exactly as they'd planned while lying together atop a horse blanket with an endless expanse of stars twinkling over them. Then, learning she was pregnant would have been something for them to discover together.

If only.

Her light-headedness was easing, though she really felt no better. But she opened her eyes and slowly pulled off the boots and socks and dropped them on the floor next to the bed. She wiggled her toes until some feeling returned and flopped back on the mattress.

The springs gave a faint squeak again.

It was a comforting sound and, too tired to even finish undressing, she dragged one of the two pillows at the head of the bed to her cheek and closed her eyes once more.

Things would be better in the morning.

They had to be.

When there were no more sounds, faint though they were, coming from his room upstairs, Quinn finally left the kitchen where he'd been hiding out. He left the house and walked back down to the barn with only the moonlight for company. He closed the door and even though there'd be endless chores to be done before the sun came up and he ought to be trying to sleep the last few hours before then, his aimless footsteps carried him even farther from the house.

But he kept glancing back over his shoulder. Looking at the dark windows on the upper story that belonged to his bedroom. Amelia had eaten the sandwich. But did that really mean anything?

If she fainted again how would he even know?

She'd been raised in the lap of luxury. First-class flights and luxury limousines driven by guys wearing suits and caps. Not economy class and bus tickets and God knew what.

Clawing his fingers through his hair, he turned back to the house. It wasn't the house that he and Jess had grown up in. That had burned nearly to the ground when Quinn was fifteen, destroying almost everything they'd owned. The same year his dad had already succeeded in literally working to death on the Rocking-U, trying to prove himself as good a rancher as the father who'd never acknowledged him. Jess, five years older, was already off and married to Mac with a baby on the way.

Ursula, his mom, would have sold off the ranch then if she'd have been able to find an interested buyer other than her dead husband's hated father. But she'd only been able to find takers for the livestock.

Despite Quinn's noisy protests, she'd moved the two of them into a two-bedroom trailer on the outskirts of town and there they'd lived until Quinn graduated from high school. Then she'd packed him off to college, packed up her clothes and moved away from the town that had only ever seemed to bring her unhappiness. Now she lived in Dallas in one of those "active adult" neighborhoods where she played bridge and tennis. She had a circle of friends she liked, and she was happy.

Not Quinn. The moment he could, he'd headed back to Horseback Hollow and the fallen-down, barren Rocking-U. He'd had a few years of college under his belt—gained only through scholarships and part-time jobs doing anything and everything he could pick up—and a new bride on his arm.

He was going to do what his father had never been able to do. Make the Rocking-U a real success.

At least one goal had been achieved.

He'd built the small house, though it had cost him two years and a wife along the way. He'd had his grandmother's piano restored and the dregs of the old, burned house hauled away. He'd shored up broken down fences and a decrepit barn. He'd built a herd. It was small, but it was prime Texas Longhorn.

He'd made something he could be proud of. Something his father had never achieved but still would have been proud of and something his father's father could choke on every time he thought about the people he liked to pretend never existed.

And when Quinn had danced with Amelia at a wedding reception six weeks ago, he'd let himself believe that there *was* a woman who could love his life the same way that he did.

All he'd succeeded in doing, though, was proving that he was Judd Drummond's son, through and through. A damn stupid dreamer.

He went back into the silent house. He had a couch in the living room. Too short and too hard to make much of a bed, but it was that or the floor. He turned off the light and sat down and worked off his boots, dropping them on the floor.

He couldn't hear anything from upstairs.

He stretched out as well as he could. Dropped his forearm over his eyes.

Listened to the rhythmic tick of the antique clock sitting on the fireplace mantel across the room.

What if she really was sick?

"Dammit," he muttered, and jackknifed to his feet. Moving comfortably in the darkness, he went to the stairs and started up. At the top, he headed to the end of the hall and closed his hand around the doorknob leading into his bedroom.

But he hesitated.

Called himself a damned fool. He ought to go back downstairs and try to redeem what little he could of the night in sleep.

Only sleeping was a laughable notion.

He'd just glance inside the room. Make sure she was sleeping okay.

He turned the knob. Nudged open the door.

He could see the dark bump of her lying, unmoving, on his bed. He stepped closer and his stockinged toes knocked into something on the floor. They bumped and thumped.

Her shoes.

It was a good thing he'd never aspired to a life of crime when he couldn't even sneak into his own bedroom without making a commotion. He'd probably been quieter when he'd found her in his damn barn.

Despite the seemingly loud noise, though, the form on the bed didn't move. He ignored the sound of his pulse throbbing in his ears until he was able to hear her soft breathing.

Fine. All good.

He had no excuse to linger. Not in a dark room in the middle of the night with another man's fiancée. There were lines a man didn't cross, and that was one of them.

It should have been easy to leave the room. And because it wasn't, he grimaced and turned.

Avoiding her shoes on the floor, he left the room more quietly than he'd entered. He returned to the couch. Threw himself down on it again.

He'd take her to her aunt's in the morning. After she woke.

And what Amelia did after that wasn't anything he was going to let himself care about.

Chapter Three

Quinn stared at the empty bed.

Amelia was gone.

It was only nine in the morning, and sometime between when he'd left the house at dawn and when he'd returned again just now, she'd disappeared.

If not for the wig that he'd found on the ground inside his barn door, he might have wondered if he'd hallucinated the entire thing.

It didn't take a genius to figure out she'd beat him to the punch in calling her aunt. One phone call to Jeanne, or to any one of the newfound cousins, and rescue would have easily arrived within an hour.

He walked into the bedroom.

The bed looked exactly the way it had when he'd tossed the quilt on top of it, before she'd gone to bed. Maybe a little neater. Maybe a lot neater.

He'd also thought her presence would linger after she was gone. But it didn't.

The room—hell, the entire house—felt deathly still. Empty.

That was the legacy she'd left that he'd have to live with.

He tossed the wig on the foot of the bed and rubbed the back of his neck. He had a crick in it from sleeping— or pretending to—on the too-short couch.

It shouldn't matter that she'd left without a word. Snuck out while his back was essentially turned. He hadn't wanted her there in the first place. And obviously, her need to "talk" hadn't been so strong, after all.

"Gone and good riddance," he muttered.

Then, because he smelled more like cow than man and Jess would give him a rash of crap about it when he showed up at his nephew's baseball game in Vicker's Corners that afternoon, he grabbed a shower and changed into clean jeans and T-shirt.

In the kitchen, the paper towel that he'd given Amelia was still sitting on the table where she'd left it, all folded up. He grabbed it to toss it in the trash, but hesitated.

She hadn't just folded the paper into a bunch of complicated triangles. She'd fashioned it into a sort of bird. As if the cheap paper towel was some fancy origami.

I have lots of useless talents.

The memory of her words swam in his head.

She'd told him that, and more, when they'd lain under the stars. How she had a degree in literature that she didn't think she'd ever use. How she spoke several languages even though she didn't much care for traveling. How she could play the piano and the harp well enough to play at some of the family's royal functions, but suffered stage fright badly enough that having to do so was agonizing.

He pinched the bridge of his nose where a pain was forming in his head and dropped the paper bird on the table again, before grabbing his Resistol hat off the peg by the back door and heading out.

He paid Tanya Fremont, one of the students where Jess and Mac taught high school, to clean his house once a week and she'd be there that weekend.

She could take care of the trash.

"Aunt Jeanne, *really?*" Amelia lifted a glossy tabloid magazine off the coffee table where it was sitting and held it up. "I can't believe you purchase these things."

Her aunt's blue eyes were wry as she sat down beside Amelia on the couch. She set the two mugs of herbal tea she was carrying on the coffee table and plucked the glossy out of Amelia's hands. She spread it over the knees of her faded blue jeans and tapped the small picture on the upper corner of the cover. "It had a picture of you and Lucie," she defended. "You and your sister looked so pretty. I thought I'd clip it out and put it in my scrapbook."

Amelia was touched by the thought even though she deplored being on the magazine cover. The photo was from the dedication of one of the orphanages her mother helped establish. Amelia recognized the dress she'd worn to the ceremony. "I don't even want to know what the article said." Undoubtedly, it had not focused on the good works of Lady Josephine or Lucie's latest accomplishments, but the pending nuptials of Amelia and Lord James Banning, the Viscount St. Allen and heir apparent to the Earl of Estingwood.

"No article," Jeanne Marie corrected. "Not really. Just a small paragraph from *close friends*—" she sketched quotes in the air "—of 'Jamelia' that the wedding date had been set, but was being kept under wraps for now to preserve your and James's privacy."

"There *is* no wedding date," Amelia blurted. She slumped back on the couch.

"Oh?" Jeanne Marie leaned forward and set the magazine on the coffee table. She picked up her tea and studied Amelia over the rim of the sturdy mug with eyes that were eerily similar to Amelia's mother.

That was to be expected, she supposed, since Josephine and Jeanne Marie were two thirds of a set of triplets. What wasn't the norm, was the fact that the siblings had only recently discovered one another. Amelia's mother hadn't even known that she'd been adopted until she'd met Jeanne Marie Fortune Jones and their triplet brother, James Marshall Fortune. He was the only reason the trio had found one another after having been separated as young children. There was even another older brother, John Fortune, to add to the new family tree.

Amelia realized her aunt wasn't gaping at her over the news there was to be no wedding. "You don't seem very surprised."

Jeanne Marie lifted one shoulder. "Well, honey. You *are* here." And again, even though her words were full of Texas drawl, her mild, somewhat ironic lilt was exactly the same as Josephine's entirely proper Brit would have been.

It was still startling to Amelia, even after meeting her aunt nearly a year ago.

"I'm assuming you have a good reason for not announcing you broke things off with your young man in England?"

"It's complicated," she murmured, even as she felt guilty for leaving her aunt under the impression that there had ever been something to break off in the first place. James had been as much a victim of their supposed engagement as she, since the presumptuous announcement had been issued by his father. But once it had been, and Amelia hadn't denied it, James had been doing his level best to convince her to make it a reality. Under immense family pressure to make a suitable marriage, he'd given up hope of a match with the girl he really loved—Astrid, who sold coffee at the stand in his building—and tried giving Amelia a family ring in hopes that she'd come around, though she'd refused to take it. "Jimmy and I have known each other a long time."

While she really only knew Quinn in the biblical sense. The irony of it all was heartbreaking.

"Sometimes a little distance has a way of uncomplicating things," Jeanne said. "And as delighted as I am to have you here, it does tend to raise a few questions. Particularly havin' to get you from Quinn Drummond's place practically before sunup. And havin' you dressed like you are."

Amelia's fingers pleated the hem of the oversize shirt. "I was trying to avoid paparazzi."

"So you said while we were driving here." Jeanne Marie finally set down the mug. She was obviously as disinterested in her tea as Amelia was. "What's going on between you and Quinn?"

"Nothing." She felt heat rise up her throat.

"And that's why you called me from his house at seven in the morning. Because nothing is going on between you two." Jeanne Marie's lips curved. "In my day, that sort of *nothing* usually led to a shotgun and a stand-up in front of a preacher whether there was another suitor in the wings or not."

Amelia winced.

Her aunt tsked, her expression going from wry to concerned in the blink of an eye. "Oh, honey." She closed her warm hands around Amelia's fidgeting fingers. "Whatever's upsetting you can be worked out. I promise you that."

Amelia managed a weak smile. "I appreciate the thought, Aunt Jeanne. But I grew up with my father always telling us not to make promises we couldn't keep."

Jeanne Marie squeezed her hand. "I wish I'd have had a chance to meet your daddy. Your mama says he was the love of her life."

Amelia nodded. Her father had died several years ago, but his loss was still sharp. "He was." She couldn't contain a yawn and covered it with her hand. Despite having slept several hours at Quinn's, she still could hardly keep her eyes open. "I'm so sorry."

"I'm the sorry one," Jeanne Marie said. She patted Amelia's hand and pushed to her feet. "You're exhausted, honey. You need to be in bed, not sitting here answering questions."

It took all the energy Amelia possessed to stand, also. "Are you certain I'm not imposing?"

Jeanne Marie laughed. "There's no such thing as imposing among family, honey. Deke and I raised seven kids in this house. Now they're all off and living their own lives. So it's nice to have one of those empty rooms filled again."

"You're very kind." She followed her aunt along the

hall and up the stairs to a corner bedroom with windows on two walls. Amelia remembered the room from her first visit to Horseback Hollow six months ago, though it had been her mother who'd been assigned to it then. It was obviously a guest room. Simply but comfortably furnished with a bed covered in a quilt with fading pastel stitching that was all the lovelier for its graceful aging, a side table with dried cat's tails sticking out of an old-fashioned milk bottle, and a sturdy oak wardrobe. White curtains, nearly translucent, hung open at the square windows and moved gently in the warm morning breeze.

"This used to be Galen's room," Jeanne Marie said. "Being the oldest, there was a time he liked lording it over the others that he had the largest room." She crossed to the windows to begin lowering the shades. "Would have put you in here back when you came for Toby's wedding in April, but James Marshall and Clara were using it."

"Leave the windows open," Amelia begged quickly. "Please."

"The sunlight won't keep you awake?"

She self-consciously tugged at her ugly shirt. Light was the least disturbing thing she could think of at the moment. And better to have sunlight than darkness while the memories of the last time she'd been at her aunt's home were caving in on her. "The breeze is too lovely to shut out."

Jeanne Marie dropped her hands. She opened the wardrobe and pulled out two bed pillows from the shelf inside and set them on the bed. "Bathroom is next door," she reminded. "I'll make sure you have fresh towels. And I'm sure that Delaney or Stacey left behind some clothes that should fit you. They might be boxed up by now, but I'll try to scare up something for you to wear once you're rested."

Her welcome was so very different than Quinn's, deserved or not, and Amelia's eyes stung.

She cried much too easily these days. "Thank you." She sat on the foot of the bed and tried not to think about sitting on the bed at Quinn's.

She'd thought that had been a guest room, too. Until she'd awakened early that morning and had gone looking for him. She'd done what she hadn't had the energy for the night before. The rooms upstairs were spacious and full of windows and nothing else. Almost like they were stuck in time. Waiting for a reason to be filled with furniture. With family. Downstairs, he had a den with a plain wooden desk and an older style computer on it. The living room had a couch, a television that looked older than the computer, and a gleaming black upright piano. She'd drawn her fingers lightly over the keys, finding it perfectly tuned.

What she hadn't found was Quinn. Not only had he been nowhere to be found inside the two-story house, but she'd seen for herself that his home possessed only a single bed.

Which, regardless of his feelings, he'd given up for her.

Jeanne Marie watched the tangled expressions crossing her new niece's delicate features and controlled the urge to take the girl into her arms and rock her just as she would have her own daughters. "We've got most of the crew coming for supper tonight. But you just come on down whenever you're ready," she said comfortingly. "And don't you worry about me spilling your personal beans to your cousins. You can do that when you're good and ready." Then she kissed Amelia's forehead and left the room, closing the door behind her.

She set out fresh towels in the bathroom, then headed downstairs to the kitchen again and stopped in surprise at the sight of her husband just coming in from the back. "I thought you'd be out all morning."

"Thought I could get the engine on that old Deere going, but I need a couple more parts." He tossed his sweat-stained cowboy hat aside and rubbed his fingers through his thick, iron-gray hair before reaching out a long arm and hooking her around the waist. "Which leaves me the chance for some morning delight with my wife before I drive over to Vicker's Corners."

Jeanne Marie laughed softly, rubbing her arms over his broad shoulders. How she loved this man who'd owned her heart from the moment they'd met. "We're not alone in the house," she warned.

His eyebrow lifted. "I didn't notice any cars out front. Who's come this early for supper? Can't be Toby and his brood." He grinned faintly. "Those kids've been coming out of their shells real nice lately."

"And they'll continue to do so," Jeanne agreed, slightly distracted by the way Deke's wide palms were drifting from her waist down over the seat of her jeans. "As long as no more hitches come up to stop Toby and Angie adopting them." Their middle son and his new wife were trying to adopt three kids he'd been fostering for the past eight months and the process hadn't exactly been smooth so far.

Her blood was turning warm and she grabbed his wide wrists, redirecting his hands to less distracting territory. "Amelia's here."

His brows pulled together for a second. "Amelia? Josephine's youngest girl?"

"We don't know another Amelia," Jeanne Marie said dryly.

His hands fell away. He leaned back against the counter and folded his arms over his chest. "Fortunes are everywhere," he murmured.

She knew his face as well as she knew her own. She had happily been Jeanne Marie Jones for forty years. But learning that she had siblings out there, learning that she had a blood connection to others in this world besides the children of his that she'd borne, had filled a void inside her that Deke had never quite been able to understand. Even though her adoptive parents had loved her, and she them, not knowing where she'd come from had always pulled at her.

And now she knew.

And though Deke hadn't protested when she'd added Fortune to her own name, she knew also that it hadn't been entirely easy for him. When their kids followed suit, it had gotten even harder for him to swallow.

No. The advent of the Fortunes to the Jones's lives hadn't been easy. And maybe it would have been easier if James had gone about things differently when he'd tracked her down. Her newfound brother was a self-made business tycoon used to having the world fall into place exactly the way he planned and he'd not only upset his own family in the process, he'd sent Jeanne Marie's family reeling, too, when he'd tried to give her part of his significant fortune.

She'd turned down the money, of course. It didn't matter to her that all of her siblings turned out to be ridiculously wealthy while she was not. She and Deke had a good life. A happy life. One blessed with invaluable wealth for the very reason that it had nothing to do with any amount of dollars and cents.

Convincing her pridefully suspicious husband that the only fortune that mattered to her was the *name* Fortune, however, had been a long process.

One that was still obviously in the works, judging by Deke's stoic expression.

"How long's she staying?" he asked.

"I have no idea. The girl came here to figure some things out, I believe." Because she always felt better being busy, she pulled a few peaches out of the basket on the counter and grabbed a knife. She'd already made a chocolate cake for dessert for that evening, but Deke always loved a fresh peach pie. And even after forty years of marriage, a man still needed to know he was in the forefront of his wife's thoughts. "Do you think she should stay somewhere else?"

He frowned quickly. "No. She's family." His eyes met hers. "I get it, Jeanne Marie."

Her faint tension eased. He might not exactly understand the way she'd taken on the Fortune name, but he did get "it" when it came to family. Nothing was more important to him, even if he didn't always have an easy time showing it.

"She'd been at Quinn Drummond's," she added. Then told him everything that had happened since Amelia had called. She pointed the tip of the paring knife she was using to peel the peaches at Deke. "I don't care what everyone's saying about her and that Banning fella." She deftly removed the peach pit and sliced the ripe fruit into a bowl. "There's definitely something going on between her and Quinn."

"I'd think Quinn's too set in his ways to be interested in a highbred filly like Amelia." Deke reached past her to filch a juicy slice. "'Specially after the merry chase that ex-wife of his led him on. She was a piece of work, remember?"

She did and she made a face. "That was years ago."

"Yup. Having your wife leave you for her old boy-friend leaves a stain, though. Least I think it would. Now he's interested in a girl the world thinks is engaged?" He stole another slice, avoiding the hand she batted at him.

"You keep eating the slices, I won't have enough left to make a pie for you," she warned.

His teeth flashed, his good humor evidently restored. He popped the morsel in his mouth and gave her a smacking kiss that tasted of him and sweet, sweet summer. It melted her heart as surely now as it had the first time he'd kissed her when they were little more than kids.

Then he grabbed his hat and plopped it on his head again. "I'll stop at the fruit stand on my way back from Vicker's Corners," he said, giving her a quick wink. "Replenish the stock." He started to push open the back screen door.

"Deke—"

He hesitated.

"You're the love of my life, you know."

His smile was slow and sweeter than the peaches. "And you're mine. That's what gets me up in the morning every day, darlin'."

Then he pushed through the screen door. It squeaked slightly, and shut with a soft slap.

Jeanne Marie pressed her hand to her chest for a moment, "Oh, my." She blew out a breath and laughed slightly at the silliness of a woman who ought to be too old for such romantic swooning.

Then she looked up at the ceiling, thinking about her young niece. Amelia was running away from something, or running to something. And she needed to figure out which it was.

Jeanne Marie was just glad that she was there to provide a resting place. And that she had a man of her own who could understand why.

Quinn had no intention of going by Jeanne Marie and Deke's place later that evening. But he ran into Deke at the tractor supply in Vicker's Corners before the baseball game and the man—typically short on words and long on hard work and honor—asked after Quinn's mom. That brief exchange of pleasantries had somehow led to Deke casually tossing out an invitation to come by for supper.

"Havin' a cookout," Deke had said. "All the kids're coming. And you know how Jeanne Marie always cooks more'n we need."

Quinn had wondered then if it was possible that Deke didn't know his wife's new niece was there. And then he had wondered if it was possible that Jeanne's new niece *wasn't* there.

Which had led to him poking at that thought all through the ball game, same way a tongue poked at a sore tooth, even though it hurt.

He ought to have just asked Deke.

Instead, here he was at six o'clock in the evening, standing there staring at the front of Jeanne and Deke's place.

He could smell grilling beef on the air and hear the high-pitched squeal of a baby laughing. Ordinarily, the smell of a steak getting seared really well would have been enough to get his boots moving. He didn't even mind the babies or the kids much. He'd had plenty of practice with Jess's batch, since she popped one out every couple of years.

His reluctance to join them now annoyed him. He'd had plenty of meals at the Jones's place over the years. He'd been in school with the older ones and counted them as friends. He'd danced at Toby's wedding. *With Amelia.* Right here, in fact, because Toby and Angie had been married out in back of the house.

Quinn hadn't been back since.

Muttering an oath, he grabbed the short-haired wig, slammed the truck door and headed around the side of the house. He knew they'd all be out back again and he was right.

This time, though, instead of rows of chairs lined up like white soldiers across the green grass and a bunch of cloth-covered tables with pretty flowers sitting on top arranged around the space, there were a couple of picnic tables covered with plastic checked tablecloths, a bunch of lawn chairs and a game of croquet in the works.

He spotted Amelia immediately and even though he wanted to pretend he hadn't been concerned about whether she had or had not sought haven with her aunt, the knot inside him eased.

She was off to one side of the grassy backyard where Toby's three kids were playing croquet, and talking with Stacey, Jeanne's and Deke's second youngest. The two females were about the same age and the same height, but Stacey was as sunny and blonde as Amelia was moon-light and brunette.

Both women were engaged, too, he thought darkly,

though only one of those engagements caused him any amount of pleasure. He was just a little surprised that Colton Foster, who was Stacey's fiancé, hadn't gotten her to the altar already. As he watched, Amelia leaned over and rubbed her nose against Piper's, Stacey's year-old daughter, who was propped on her mama's hip.

He looked away and aimed toward Deke where he and Liam were manning the grill. "Smells good," he greeted. "Would only smell better if that was Rocking-U beef."

Liam snorted good-naturedly. Horseback Hollow was dotted with small cattle ranches and all of them were more supportive than competitive with each other. "You got yourself a new pet there? Looks like a rat."

Quinn wished he'd have left the wig in the truck. He'd only thought as far as returning it to its owner so he wouldn't have the reminder around. He hadn't thought about the questions that doing so would invite. "It's a wig. Thought maybe one of Toby's kids might want to keep it around for Halloween or something." The excuse was thin and he knew it. "My sister's kids outgrew it, I guess," he improvised and felt stupid even as he did. He'd never developed a taste for lying. Anyone who knew Jess's brood would also know the five boys were hellions who wouldn't be caught dead wearing a wig.

Liam was eying him oddly, too. "Whatever, man." He grabbed a beer from an ice-filled barrel and tossed it to him. "Crack that open and get started. Maybe it'll soften you up before we get to dickering over that bull of yours I want to buy."

Despite everything, Quinn smiled. He tossed the wig on one of the picnic benches nearby. "Rocky's not for sale, my friend."

"Even if I paid you twice what he's worth?"

They'd had this debate many times. Quinn knew Liam wouldn't overpay and Liam knew Quinn wasn't selling, anyway. "That bull's semen's worth gold to me."

"Oh." The word was faint, brief and still filled with some shock.

The knots tightened inside him again and Quinn turned to see Amelia standing beside him.

Chapter Four

Her fragility struck Quinn all over again, like a fist in his gut.

The red dress that she was wearing was pretty enough, he guessed. But it was loose. And the straps over her shoulders couldn't hide the way her collarbones were too prominent.

She looked like she needed to sit at a table and stuff herself for a month of Sundays.

As if she read his disapproving thoughts, her cheeks were nearly as red as the dress.

The day of Toby's wedding, she'd worn a strapless ice-blue dress that ended just above her perfect knees, and a weird little puff of some feathery thing on her head. When they'd ended up sneaking off for a drive in his truck, he'd teased her about it. She'd promptly tugged it off, and plopped his cowboy hat on her head, where it had slipped down over her eyes, and said she was in the market for a new look, anyway.

His lips twisted, his eyes meeting hers. "You're going to hear words like *bull's semen* if you're going to play around cowboys, princess."

Stacey, standing beside Amelia, rolled her eyes. "Good grief, Quinn. Manners much?"

"It's quite all right," Amelia said quickly. She lifted her chin a little. "This is Texas, for goodness' sake. Cattle ranch country. I certainly don't imagine anyone stands around discussing tea and biscuits. Or, cookies, I guess you call them."

He nearly choked. Because they'd laughed together about that, too. Only she'd been naked at the time, and throatily telling him that she'd bet he'd enjoy teatime perfectly well if she served it up for him after making love.

"Depends on whose cookies you're talking about," Deke said. "Jeanne Marie makes some oatmeal peanut-butter deals that are the talk of three counties." His dry humor broke the faint tension. "Stacey girl, you wanna grab a tray for these steaks? They're 'bout ready."

"Sure."

"I'll take her," Amelia offered quickly, reaching out her hands for Piper, and Stacey handed her over. She settled the wide-eyed toddler on her hip and tickled her cheek, making Piper squeal and wriggle. "Who is the prettiest baby girl here, hmm?"

For some reason, Quinn's neck prickled.

He twisted the cap off his beer and focused on Liam. "Where's your better half, anyway?" There was no sign of his friend's red-haired fiancée.

"Julia's meeting with one of the suppliers over at the Cantina. She'll be here as soon as she finishes up."

"Is the restaurant still going to open on schedule?" Amelia asked.

Liam nodded. "Two weeks from now, right on track."

The Hollows Cantina was a big deal for their little town. It was owned and to be operated by Marcos Mendoza and his wife, Wendy Fortune Mendoza, who'd relocated all the way from Red Rock, a good four hundred Texas miles away. They'd hired Julia as an assistant manager and the establishment promised upscale dining that was intended to draw not only the locals from Horseback Hollow and nearby Vicker's Corners, but as far away as Lubbock. Considering the Mendozas' success with Red, a fancy Mexican food restaurant in Red Rock that was famous even beyond the state lines, Quinn figured they had a decent shot of success at it.

He was reserving judgment on whether that all would be a good thing for Horseback Hollow or not. He wasn't vocally opposed to it like some folks, nor was he riding around on the bandwagon of supporters, though he was glad enough for Julia. She'd always been a hard worker and deserved her shot as much as anyone did.

He, personally, would probably still choose the Horseback Hollow Grill over the Cantina. Even on a good day, he wasn't what he would call "upscale" material.

"My mother has the grand opening on her calendar," Amelia said. "I know she's looking forward to it. Not only is Uncle James going to be there, but Uncle John, as well. It should be quite a family reunion."

Quinn stopped pretending an interest in his beer and looked at her. Ironically, the British Fortunes seemed too upscale for the Cantina. "And you? Is it on your calendar, too, princess? Maybe you'll drag your fiancé along for the trip."

Amelia's chocolate-brown eyes went from her cousin's face to Quinn's and for the first time since he'd met her, they contained no emotion whatsoever. "I'm not sure what I'll be doing by the end of the month." Her voice was smoothly pleasant and revealed as little as her eyes did.

Her "royal face," he realized.

She'd talked about having one. Having had to develop as a little girl the ability to give nothing away by expression, deed or word.

He'd just never seen it in person before. And not directed at him.

Piper was wriggling on her hip and Amelia leaned over to set the little girl on her feet. She kept hold of Piper's tiny hands as the girl made a beeline toddle for the wig sitting on the picnic bench next to them.

"Keekee," she chortled, and reached for the wig.

Amelia laughed lightly and scooped up the wig before Piper could reach it and brushed the short thick strands against the baby's face. "That's not a kitty, darling. It's a wig."

She'd crouched next to Piper and while the child chortled over the hairy thing, she glanced up at Quinn. "There was no need to return the wig to me, Quinn," she told him. "You could have tossed it in the trash bin."

He really wished he would have.

Liam tilted his beer to his lips but not quickly enough to hide his faint grin. "Thought the rat belonged to your sis's kids."

"Here's the tray," Stacey announced, striding up with a metal cookie sheet in her hand that she set on the side of the grill.

She was also carrying a big bowl of coleslaw under

her other arm, and, glad of an escape route, Quinn slid his hand beneath it. "I'll put it on the table before you drop it." He turned away from the lot of them and carried it over to a folding table that had obviously been set out to hold the food.

Trying not to watch Quinn too openly, Amelia continued entertaining the sweet baby with the wig while everyone else seemed to suddenly spring into action organizing the food onto plates and the people onto picnic benches.

Though she tried to avoid it, she somehow found herself sitting directly across from Quinn. He was hemmed in on one side by Delaney, Jeanne Marie and Deke's youngest daughter, and Liam on the other. Amelia was caught between Jeanne Marie and Deke.

If she didn't know better, she almost would have suspected her aunt and uncle of planning it.

Judging by the way Quinn noticeably ignored her, he was no more comfortable with the seating plan than she was. Fortunately, his friendship with Liam was evident as the two men dickered over the issue of Rocky's studding abilities and whether or not the summer season would be wetter or drier than usual.

"Have some more corn bread," Jeanne Marie said, nudging a basket of the fragrant squares into her hands.

Amelia obediently put another piece on her plate, and managed a light laugh when Deke tried to talk her into another steak, though she'd only eaten a fraction of the one on her plate. "If I ate all this, I'd pop," she protested.

"So, Amelia," Delaney drew her attention. "What are you doing in Horseback Hollow, anyway?" Her eyes were bright with curiosity as she grinned. "Are you planning some secret meeting with your wedding gown designer? Texas has our very own Charlene Dalton. She's based in Red Rock and I hear she did Emily Fortune's gown."

"Delaney," Jeanne Marie tsked, handing the corn bread across to her daughter. "You're sounding like one of those nosy reporters."

Delaney made a protesting sound. "That's not fair. None of us expected to find ourselves family with *The* Fortunes. If you can't share some secrets among your own family, who can you share 'em with? It's not like I'll go tattling to the newspapers. And besides. I didn't get to see Emily's gown outside of pictures, 'cause she got married before we even knew we all were cousins!"

"It's all right," Amelia said quickly. Not only could she sense her aunt's sudden discomfort, but she was painfully aware of Quinn across from her. "I'm not...not planning any designer sessions." She was loath to discuss her personal business in front of everyone, even if they *were* family. That just wasn't the way she'd been raised. Even among her four brothers and sister, she didn't get into whys and wherefores and the most personal of emotions. She hadn't even divulged all the facts to her own mother about her "engagement," though she knew Josephine had her suspicions.

She tried not looking at Quinn, but couldn't help herself. "I'm not planning anything." It wasn't exactly a public admission, but since she'd discovered she was pregnant with his child, it was entirely truthful.

"'Scuse me." He suddenly rose and extricated himself from the picnic bench and the human bookends holding him there.

Amelia's fingernails dug into her palms as she

watched him carry his plate over to the table of food and make a point of studying the display.

"Getting a microphone stuck in your face or a camera flash blinding you every time you go out in public would be a pain in the butt," Deke said, as if nothing had happened. Then he looked around at the silence his unexpected input drew. His eyebrows rose. "Well. Would be," he drawled in conclusion.

And that seemed to be that.

Nobody else broached the subject about Amelia's unplanned appearance. Nor did the topic of the wedding come up again.

And Quinn never returned to their picnic table.

He stuck around long enough to have a piece of the three-layer chocolate cake when Jeanne Marie presented it, along with a peach pie that was so picturesque it might have come out of the kitchens at the Chesterfield estate. But whenever Amelia entered his vicinity, he exited hers.

It was so plainly obvious that he was avoiding her that she felt herself receiving looks of sympathy from Stacey, Delaney *and* Liam's fiancée, Julia, who'd arrived in time for dessert.

She didn't want sympathy.

She wanted Quinn's love.

In the absence of that, at least his understanding.

But clearly he wasn't going to offer that, either.

She saw him shake Deke's hand, drop a kiss on her aunt's cheek and exchange easily a half-dozen goodbyes with some of the others, without a single glance her way. And then he was walking away, heading out of sight around the corner of her aunt's house.

She swallowed and sucked all of her feelings inward until she felt reasonably confident that her expression was calm. She listened in on Toby and Angie's conversation as they talked about the difficulties they kept encountering trying to adopt the three Hemings children Toby had been fostering ever since she'd first met him, and knew she made the appropriate nods and sounds when she should have. But a portion of her mind was wondering if she could get back home again without drawing undue media attention.

Which was rather laughable to worry about now.

The attention she'd draw once word of her pregnancy got out would thoroughly eclipse what she'd already garnered.

And poor James. Instead of dealing with the embarrassment of a broken engagement, he would have to endure speculation over being the baby's father. It wouldn't matter that he wasn't. It wouldn't matter what statements were issued or what proof was given.

Forever on, people would whisper. Every time either one of them did something to draw the attention of the media, the scandal would be dug up all over again, regurgitated on the internet or on gossip networks.

They'd all pay the price and none more dearly than her and Quinn's innocent baby.

Her head swam dizzily and she excused herself, walking blindly. She instinctively followed the path that Quinn had taken, heading around the side of the house and away from all of the noisy gaiety.

Going home was as impossible as staying in Horseback Hollow would be.

The thought came over her in a wave and her knees went weak. She stopped, bracing herself with one hand against the side of the house.

"Are you going to pass out again?"

She nearly jumped out of her skin at the sound of Quinn's voice. He was standing a few feet away, his hazel eyes alert, as though he was ready to leap forward if he had to.

At least he didn't hate her badly enough to allow her to collapse flat on her face.

She let out a choking laugh at the thought, which only had him closing the distance between them, his expression even warier as he clasped her bare arms.

She shivered, looking up into his face. The night they'd danced, she'd felt as if they'd known one another for all their lives. "I think I'm losing my mind, Quinn." Even her voice sounded unhinged, shaking and pitched too high.

He made a rough sound. "You're not losing your mind."

Where was her dignity? Her self-control? Her throat tightened even more, her voice almost a squeak. "But you don't know—"

"Shh." His big warm hand slid around the back of her neck and he pulled her against his chest in a motion that felt both reluctant and desperate. "You're going to make yourself collapse again. Is that what you want?"

Her forehead rubbed against the front of his soft plaid shirt as she shook her head. She could feel the heat of his hard chest burning through the cotton. Could hear the rhythmic beat of his heart when she turned her cheek against him.

He was holding her, though not cradling her. But her ragged emotions didn't care. They only wanted her to burrow against him while he safely held everything that didn't matter at bay.

She'd never felt even a fraction of this need when she

was with James. If only she had, things wouldn't be in such a mess.

Her fingers twisted into Quinn's shirt lapel. "There's something I need to tell you."

"Well it's gonna have to wait." His hands tightened around her arms as he forcibly set her back a foot. "I only came back to warn you that there's an SUV parked maybe a hundred yards down the road that's not from around here. Has a rental car sticker on the bumper." His fingertips pressed into her flesh and his gaze, as it roved over her face, was shuttered once more. "It's probably nothing, but the strangers that've been coming around the Hollow these days usually stick to town. They don't traipse out onto private property and park off the side of the road half-hidden behind the bushes."

She grasped at the shreds of her composure and came up with threads. His thumbs were rubbing back and forth over her upper arms and she wondered if he even realized it. "You think it's a reporter." Maybe even that dreadful Ophelia Malone had managed to catch up to her. The young paparazzo had sprung from nowhere after Amelia's "engagement" and seemed determined to earn her stripes on Amelia ever since.

"All I'm thinking is that the car doesn't belong." His thumbs stopped moving. He still held her arms to steady her, yet managed to put another few inches between them. "But I don't figure any of the Joneses—*Fortune* Joneses," he corrected himself, "deserve their lives intruded upon."

"Whereas this Fortune Chesterfield does?"

His lips twisted and his brows lowered. "Don't make me feel sorry for you, princess."

"I'm not trying to!" Despair congealed inside her

chest and she lifted her palms to his face. She felt his sudden stillness and mindlessly stepped closer. "Please give me a chance to make things right, Quinn." Feeling as powerless as a moth flying into a flame, she stretched up on the toes of her borrowed sandals and pressed her mouth to his jaw. The hard angle felt bristly against her lips. "That's all I want. A chance." She stretched even farther, pulling on his shoulders, until her lips could reach his.

And for a moment, a sweet moment that sent her hopes spinning, he kissed her back.

But then he jerked away.

His hands felt like iron as he held her in place and took another step back, putting distance between them yet again. "Finish making one bed before you try getting in another." His voice was low. Rough.

"I was never in James's bed," she whispered. Her lips still tingled. "I'm not in it now. What can I do to make you believe me?"

A muscle worked in his jaw. "Walk out to that SUV and see if it's a reporter, and if it is, tell 'em what you told me. That the two of you aren't engaged. Never were."

She swallowed. "And that would make everything all right? Between you and me?"

He didn't answer and her stomach sank right back to her toes.

Of course it wouldn't.

He'd made up his mind where she was concerned and that was the end of it.

It didn't matter who was to blame for what as far as the "engagement" was concerned. James's father had precipitated everything by announcing they were engaged.

And she'd compounded the problem by not denying it when she could have.

By talking to the paparazzi now, all she would succeed in doing would be hurting James, embarrassing his family, and by extension, her own.

And in the process, she wouldn't gain a thing where Quinn was concerned.

She drew herself up. Lifted her chin. She was a Chesterfield. A Fortune Chesterfield. Even if her world was disintegrating around her, she needed to remember that fact. "That would be throwing James to the wolves."

His eyes flattened even more. "So?"

She exhaled, praying for strength. It was obvious that he wouldn't welcome hearing any defense of the other man. "An announcement like that needs to come through official channels, not some random gossipmonger on the side of the road. *Don't!*" She stared him down. "Don't look at me like that. Whether you want to believe me or not, it's true. Otherwise it would be just one more rumor tossing around among the flotsam."

"Even though it came from you."

She nodded. "Even though." This time, she was the one to put more space between them, though she had to force herself to do it. But it was enough to make his hands finally fall away from her arms. It took every speck of self-control she possessed not to clasp her arms around herself to hold in the feel of his touch. "James and I had been dating nearly a year when you and I—" She drew in a shuddering breath. "When I came here for Toby's wedding," she amended. "The…advantages of us marrying had come up a few times. I never lied to you about that."

"No, princess. Your lie was in pretending you weren't

going to bring those advantages to reality. You said you weren't in love with him. And that I did believe. Or there's no way we'd have ended up out in that field that night." His lips thinned. "Wouldn't have happened."

"Are you trying to convince me of that or yourself?"

The muscle in his jaw flexed. Once. Twice. Then it went still. His expression turned stoic and he didn't speak.

She realized she'd pressed her hands to her stomach and made herself stop. "And…and after I went back home to all that—" she waved her hand, trying to encompass the indescribable media storm that had greeted her "—and you made it plain once you finally deigned to speak with me that there was no…no hope for us—" Her voice broke and she stopped again, gathering herself. "James suggested we go on with the illusion. His father is in very poor health. For an assortment of reasons, he wants to see James married and pass on his title to him while he's still alive. We weren't the great romance everyone wants to make us out to be, but we *were* friends and, given time, he hoped we might be more." Her vision glazed with tears as she stared at him. "I didn't have you. So, yes. I made no public contradictions. I'd had one night of magic and I let it slip through my fingers. Maybe a life with him was the best I could expect after that. But then I—"

"Enough!" He slashed his hand through the air between them. "Enough of the fairy-tale bull, princess. I've been down this road before. I already know how it goes." His smile was cold and cutting. "I made the mistake of marrying the last woman who was selling a story like this. I am not in the market to buy it again."

Then, while she was frozen in speechless shock, he turned on his boot heel and strode back to his truck parked nearby.

Chapter Five

The next morning it was Quinn's sister, Jess, who saw the photograph first.

It was grainy. It had obviously been taken from a considerable distance and the subjects' faces weren't entirely visible, or even entirely clear.

But it was enough for Jess.

She slapped the piece of paper on Quinn's kitchen table in front of him and jabbed her finger at the image. "That's you." She jabbed again. "That's Amelia." Then she propped her hands on her hips and stuck her face close to his, wholly, righteously in big-sister mode. "What the *hell*, Quinn? They've already coined a nickname for you!"

Annoyed, because even though she was five years his senior, he was a grown man and not in the least interested in being called on her metaphorical carpet, he pushed her aside and picked up the sheet of paper that she'd obviously printed off her computer. "They who?"

Her arms flapped as she gaped at him. "It doesn't matter who! You've got eyes. You can read reasonably well, last time I checked. The caption is right there!"

Is this the end for Jamelia? Who is the tall, dark Horseback Hollow Homewrecker caught in a passionate clinch with England's own runaway bride?

He let out a disgusted sound and crumpled the thin paper in his fist. "You have five kids, a husband and a full-time job at the high school. When the hell do you have time for hunting up this sort of crap on the internet?"

"Summer vacation," she returned. "And obviously you've never acquainted yourself with internet alerts." She waved her cell phone that she seemed perpetually attached to under his nose, then shoved it back in her pocket.

He wasn't sure if she was more disgusted with the photograph itself or with his seeming ineptitude where technology was concerned. The only thing he kept a computer for was ranch records and he detested using it even for that. He'd rather be out in the open air than sitting in the office pecking at computer keys.

"That picture is everywhere," she added. "All this time and you never said *anything* about her to me! How long has this been going on?"

"There's no *this*." He opened the cupboard door beneath the sink and pushed the wad of paper deep into the trash can stored there.

"Please. Don't try saying that isn't you and Amelia in the picture. Where were you, anyway?"

Standing to one side of the Joneses' house, not as hidden from view as he'd thought.

He didn't voice the words. Just eyed his sister. "It's Saturday morning," he said instead. "Shouldn't you be at a soccer game or something instead of cornering me in my own kitchen?"

She pointed her finger at him, giving him the stink eye that she'd had perfected since she was a superior eight years old and didn't like him coming uninvited into her room anymore. "She's an engaged woman, Quinn."

It wasn't anything he didn't know and hadn't been tarring himself for. But that didn't mean he welcomed his sister's censure, too. And, he justified to himself, the photograph hadn't caught him kissing Amelia; it had caught *her* kissing *him*. "Engaged isn't married."

He scooped up a Texas Rangers ball cap and tugged it down over his eyes before shoving through the wood-framed screen door leading outside. For her, Saturdays were chock-full of squiring one kid or another hither and yon.

For him, Saturdays meant the same chores that every other day meant and he fully intended on getting to them. If he kept acting normal, sooner or later, things would be normal. It had worked that way when Carrie left. He had to believe it would work again now, or he might as well order up a straightjacket, size extra-large-tall, right now.

Amelia woke early the next day after yet another fitful night of sleep. She could smell the heady aroma of coffee wending its way from downstairs and she rolled out of bed, donning the robe that Jeanne Marie had loaned her. Downstairs, she found her aunt sitting at the kitchen table. Her silver hair—usually pinned up—was hanging in a long braid down her back and she had a pair of reading glasses perched on her nose as she perused a newspaper.

When Amelia walked into the room, she looked over the top of her eyeglasses and smiled. "Aren't you the early bird this morning," she greeted. "Would you like coffee?"

Amelia waved her aunt back into her seat when she started to rise. "Don't get up." She wanted coffee in the worst way, but had read that caffeine was something pregnant women were supposed to avoid. "Water's all I want." To prove it, she pulled a clean glass out of the dish rack where several had been turned upside down after being washed, and filled it from the tap. Then she sat down across from her aunt. She was determined not to think about Quinn for the moment.

She'd spent enough time doing that when she'd been unable to sleep. She'd thought about him. And the fact that he'd once been married. Something he hadn't shared before at all.

"I need some clothes of my own," she said. "I can't keep borrowing." It was something she'd never done in her entire life. And she needed underwear. She'd been washing her silk knickers every night, but enough was enough.

"Well." Jeanne Marie looked amused. "You can, you know. But a pretty girl like you doesn't want to keep walking around in things two sizes too large." She adjusted her glasses and glanced at her newspaper again. "Guess you already know you won't find much in the way of clothes shopping here in Horseback Hollow."

"I know." Much as she loved the area, Horseback Hollow only consisted of a few small businesses. "I thought perhaps Vicker's Corners." She hadn't been to the nearby town, but she'd heard mention of it often enough and knew it was only twenty miles away. "When I was talking to Stacey yesterday, she mentioned that there are a few shops there."

"Yes," Jeanne Marie agreed. "You'll find more of a selection in Lubbock, though."

She didn't want to go to Lubbock. She wanted to avoid all towns of any real size. Vicker's Corners was probably pushing it as it was. "I just need a few basics," she said. "I'm sure Vicker's Corners will suit." She chewed the inside of her lip for a moment. "I also ought to purchase a cell phone." Molly had called it "a burner." One that nobody—namely Ophelia Malone and her ilk—would know to track. "Do you think I'd be able to find one there, as well?"

"Imagine so. There's a hardware store that carries everything from A to Z." Jeanne Marie turned the last page of the newspaper and folded it in half. "I'd drive you myself, but I have to go to a baby shower my friend Lillian is giving her niece this afternoon. I can call one of the kids or Deke to drive you."

"I don't want to put anyone out." She'd sprung her "visit" on them uninvited. She certainly didn't expect them to rearrange their plans because of her. "I don't suppose I could hire a car around here? I have some experience driving in other countries."

Jeanne Marie's smile widened. "We're not exactly blessed with car rental companies," she said mildly. "But if you want to drive yourself, there's no problem. You can use my car and drop me off at Lillian's. Her place is on the way to Vicker's Corners."

Amelia hesitated. "I don't know, Aunt Jeanne. It's one thing to rent a car, but to impose—"

Her aunt waved her hand. "Oh, hush up on that imposition nonsense, would you please? Would you think your cousins were imposing if they came over to England to visit y'all there?"

"Of course not."

"This is about money, then."

Dismayed, Amelia quickly shook her head. "No," she lied. Because it was exactly about money. Her aunt and uncle had an undeniably modest lifestyle in comparison to the Chesterfields. The whole lot of Jeanne and Deke's family could visit their estate and they'd still have room to spare.

Jeanne Marie just eyed her.

Amelia's shoulders drooped. "Mum'll want to put me in chains if I've offended you."

Her aunt's lips twitched. "I'm not offended, Amelia," she assured. She propped her elbows on the table and folded her hands together, leaning toward her. "There are all kinds of wealth, honey. I have no problem whatsoever with the type of wealth I've been blessed with. I love my life exactly the way it is. A husband who loves me, kids we both adore and the opportunity to see them starting on families of their own. Just because we're not millionaires like my brothers and sister, doesn't mean we don't have all that we need." She tapped her fingertip on the table and her eyes crinkled. "And if I want to lend my niece my car, I will."

Amelia studied her for a moment. "Did you always know that this was the life you wanted?"

"Pretty much. I was only twenty-two, but I knew I wanted to marry Deke almost as soon as I met him." She chuckled. "Depending on the day, he might not necessarily admit to the same thing."

Her chest squeezed. She'd felt the same way about Quinn. "I'm a year older than you were then, and I don't feel half the confidence you must have felt."

Jeanne Marie rose and began puttering around the kitchen. She was wearing an oversize plaid shirt that looked like it was probably Deke's and a pair of jeans cut off at the knees. "Comparing us is as silly as comparing apples and oranges, sweetheart. I was learning how to be a good rancher's wife. You're out there establishing orphanages and dedicating hospital wings and such."

"Mummy's the one who gets those things done. I just—" She broke off and sighed. "I don't know what I just do." She made a face. "Maybe the media's right and the only thing I was perfectly suited for was being a proper wife for the future Earl of Estingwood."

"Which you've already admitted you're not planning to do," Jeanne reminded. "So *you* know you're not suited."

Her aunt had no idea just how unsuited.

She rose and restlessly tightened the belt of her borrowed flannel robe. "You really don't mind lending me your vehicle?"

Jeanne Marie smiled. "Just make sure you drive on the right side of the road."

Unfortunately, after Amelia had let off her aunt later that afternoon at her friend's home, she discovered driving on the right side was a task easier said than done.

Her aunt had told her that it was a straight shot down the roadway to Vicker's Corners. What she hadn't said was that the roadway wasn't, well, *straight*.

It was full of curves and bumps and dips and even

though there was hardly any other traffic to speak of, more than once Amelia found herself wanting to drift to the other side of the road.

By the time she made it to the quaintly picturesque little town of Vicker's Corners, her hands ached from clenching the steering wheel so tightly, and she heartily wished she'd just have waited until her aunt was available to bring her into town.

Which was such a pathetic, spoiled thought that she was immediately disgusted with herself. Back home, more often than not, she used the services of a driver. It was simpler. And as Jimmy had so often told her, it was safer.

But that privilege also came as part and parcel along with public eyes following her activities. And that was something she'd always hated. Growing up was difficult enough without having an entire country witnessing your missteps.

She didn't care what the supposed advantages were of being raised a Chesterfield. No matter what happened with Quinn, she was not going to raise their child in that sort of environment. It was fine for some.

But not for her. Not for her baby.

When she saw the way several cars were parked, nose in to the curb between slanted lines, she pulled into the first empty space she spotted and breathed out a sigh of relief. She locked up the car and tucked the keys inside the pocket of her borrowed sundress. It was the same red one from the day before because the other clothes from Stacey and Delaney that Jeanne Marie had found had been from their earlier years. It was either wear the slightly oversize sundress once more, or skintight jeans and T-shirts with the names of rock bands splashed in glitter across her breasts.

Even though she was the only one who cared about what she wore, the sundress was preferable.

Looking up and down the street, Amelia mentally oriented herself with the descriptions that Jeanne Marie had given her of the town. Her impetuously chosen parking spot was directly in front of the post office. Across the street and down a bit was the three-story bed and breakfast, identifiable by the green-and-white-striped awnings her aunt had described. Which meant that around the corner and down the block, she would find the hardware store her aunt recommended.

She waited for two cars to pass, then headed across the street. Her first task would be to secure a phone and then she'd check in with her mother. Amelia had instructed Molly to let Josephine know her plans once she'd left the country.

It wasn't that she'd been afraid her mum would talk her out of going. It was that Amelia didn't entirely trust everyone on her mother's staff to have the same discretion that Molly did. Someone had been feeding that Malone woman details concerning Amelia's schedule and the only ones who kept a copy were her mother's staff and James's assistant.

She reached the hardware store and went inside. There was a girl manning a cash register near the front door and she barely gave Amelia a look as she continued helping a customer, so Amelia set off to find what she needed.

The aisles were narrow; the shelves congested with everything from hammers and industrial-sized paint thinners to cookware. But she didn't see any electronics. She returned to the clerk who'd finished with the customer. "Do you offer cell phones?"

The girl chewed her gum and looked up from the magazine lying open on the counter. "Yeah." She jerked her chin. "Over on aisle—" She broke off, her eyes suddenly widening. "Hey, aren't you that fancy chick related to Jeanne Jones who's marrying this guy?" She lifted the magazine and tapped a photo of James Banning astride one of his polo ponies, his mallet midswing. "He is *so* hot."

"Jeanne Marie is my aunt." She managed a calm smile. "The phones?"

"Oh, yeah. Right." The girl slid off her stool and came around the counter. "I'll show you." She headed toward the rear of the store. "Keep alla that stuff on this aisle over here 'cause the only way out is back past the counter. Cuts down on shoplifting." She gave Amelia a quick look. "Not saying *you* would—"

"I know you're not." Amelia spotted several older-style cell phones hanging from hooks. They were generations away from the fancy device she was used to using. But then that fancy thing had been hacked.

She grabbed the closest phone. It was packaged in the kind of tough, clear plastic that always seemed impossible to open.

The girl snapped her gum. "Are you gonna want a phone card, too?" She gestured at the rack next to the small phone selection. It held an array of colorful credit-card-sized cards. "You pay for the minutes up front," she added at Amelia's blank look. "You know. Otherwise you gotta get a contract and all that."

Feeling foolish, Amelia studied the cards for a moment. Contracts were certainly something to avoid. "Do they cover international calls?"

"Yeah." The girl looked over her head when a jangling bell announced the arrival of another customer. Then she tapped one of the cards. "That one's the best value for your money," she provided as she backed away. "I've gotta get back to the register," she excused herself.

"Thank you." Amelia looked at the display. She wasn't going to use her credit card. Just the cash. Which meant, for now at any rate, she needed to use it wisely. She chose the card the girl suggested and flipped it over, reading the tiny print on the back. Not once in her life had she ever needed to concern herself with such details.

She carried the phone and the card back to the register, but stopped short at the sight of the young blonde woman standing there with the clerk.

Ophelia Malone.

Amelia ducked back in the aisle with the cell phones where she couldn't be seen. There was country music playing over a speaker and she couldn't hear what they were saying, but she didn't need to. There was only one reason why Ophelia would be in that store at that moment and Amelia was it.

She quickly returned the phone and the card to their places on the racks and scurried around the opposite end of the aisle, looking for an escape even though the girl had said there wasn't another way out. She discovered the reason quickly enough. There *was* another exit. But it was a fire exit and she knew from regrettable experience in similar situations that going through it would set off an alarm. Gnawing on her lip, she edged to the end of the aisle again and peeked around the racks toward the front.

Ophelia wasn't there. But the door hadn't jangled, meaning she was still in the store somewhere.

She felt like the fox in a hunt and that never ended well for the fox. She continued sneaking her way around the aisles, keeping to the ends because there was less chance of getting caught, hearing the door jangling periodically. When the urge to look grew too great, she held her breath, darting up the empty row next to her where she could see the entrance just as another customer came in.

She quickly backed out of sight again, then nearly jumped out of her skin when the clerk appeared.

"There you are," she said. "Your friend's looking for you."

"She's not my friend," she corrected, keeping her voice low. Feeling increasingly hemmed in, she grabbed the clerk's hands and the girl's eyes widened. "She can't find me. Is there another way out or an office where I can wait until she's gone?"

"Too late, Lady Chesterfield." Ophelia stepped into sight. Her green eyes were as sharp as her smile, and in a move she'd probably practiced from the womb, she deftly lifted her camera out of her purse.

Chapter Six

Amelia could hear the clicking whirr of the shutter even before the lens aimed her way and she wanted to scream in frustration.

"Any comments on Mr. Tall, Dark and Nameless you were kissing yester—" Ophelia broke off when a shrieking alarm blasted through the store, making all three of them jump. "What the bloody hell is *that?*"

"The fire alarm." The salesclerk waved her hands, looking panicked. "You have to leave the store."

"Oh, come on," Ophelia said impatiently.

"There are flammable items everywhere, ma'am. We don't take chances." The clerk pushed the reporter toward the aisle where a half-dozen other customers were jostling around the displays in the narrow aisle toward the front door.

Seizing the opportunity, Amelia dashed instead for

the fire exit in the rear. The alarm was going off already so what did it matter?

She hit the bar on the door and it flew open, banging against the wall behind it, and she darted out into an alleyway. Her heart pounding, she shoved the door closed behind her. The fire alarm was noisy even through the door, pulsing in the air and making it difficult to think straight. Could she make it back to Aunt Jeanne's car without Ophelia seeing her?

"Hey. Over here." A tall, dark-haired woman dressed in cutoffs and a tank top beckoned from one side near a large, metal trash bin. "They won't see you over here."

Amelia's didn't stop to question the assistance and her sandals slipped on the rough pavement as she took off toward her. She caught herself from landing on her bottom and hurried, half jogging, half skipping after her rescuer who set off briskly away from the hardware store. "*You* set off the alarm?"

"Yes, but if they try to fine me for it, I'm denying it. Already had to pay a few of them thanks to my oldest boy." They reached the end of the alley and the woman held up a warning hand as she cautiously checked the street. A fire truck, siren blaring and lights flashing, roared past. She waited a moment, then beckoned. "Come on. You need to get off the street before more people see you."

"How'd you—"

"Never mind." The woman grabbed her arm and tugged her out into the open. Amelia could see her aunt's car still parked in front of the post office down the street, but they didn't head that way. Instead, the woman pulled Amelia through the propped-open door of the bed-and-breakfast.

A teenager wielding a dust cloth across a fake Chippendale desk looked at them, clearly surprised. "Mrs. O'Malley. What're you doing—" her eyes landed on Amelia and widened with recognition "—here," she finished faintly. She pointed her dust rag at Amelia. "You're...you—"

"Yes, yes. She's her." The brunette—Mrs. O'Malley, obviously—nudged the teen's shoulder to gain her attention again. "You have any guests today, Shayla?"

Shayla shook her head and her wildly curling orangey-red ponytail bounced. "Not yet, but Ma's expecting some newlyweds t'night."

Mrs. O'Malley boldly stepped around the desk and grabbed an old-fashioned hotel key off a hook. "Gonna use number three for a while, then. Keep quiet about that, though, if anyone comes asking, all right?"

Shayla's lips moved, but no words came.

"All right?"

The ponytail bounced again, this time with Shayla's jerky nod. "Yes, ma'am."

"Good girl. Now come on." Mrs. O'Malley tugged Amelia toward a lovely staircase with a white painted banister and dark stained wood treads and started up. "Shayla's a student of mine," she said over her shoulder. "Her mother owns this place."

Thoroughly discomfited, Amelia followed. "You're a teacher?"

"High school English." The other woman turned on the landing and headed up another flight, her pace never slowing. "Better hurry your tush, hon," she advised.

Amelia grasped the banister and quickened her pace. Her head was pounding from the adrenaline rush. "Why did you set off the alarm?"

"Figured somebody needed to do something." She glanced over her shoulder. "I went in to buy paint for my youngest's room—the sweetest shade of pink you ever saw—and I saw that woman showing Katie your picture and asking about you."

"I should have tried Lubbock," Amelia muttered.

"You didn't get your paint and I didn't get my phone." They'd reached the top of the stairs and Mrs. O'Malley unlocked the only door there, pushing it open to reveal a cozy-looking guest suite.

They went inside and Mrs. O'Malley immediately crossed to the mullioned window and looked out. "Talk about the nick of time," she said.

Amelia shut the door before joining her, and keeping to one side of the window, looked down. She could see Ophelia marching up the street, her stride determined as she systematically went in and out the doors of each business until she disappeared beneath the striped awning over the B and B's front door.

Hoping she hadn't jumped from the pot into the fire, Amelia sank down on a white wicker rocking chair situated near the window and eyed the other woman. "What do you want out of this? If it's money, you'll be sorely disappointed. My family's dealt with more embarrassing situations than shopping for a discount cell phone."

Mrs. O'Malley didn't look calculating, though. If anything, her light brown eyes turned pitying. "Never heard of a Good Samaritan?"

Amelia's lips twisted. "I apologize for my suspicions, but lately helpful strangers have been in rather short supply."

The woman sat on the corner of the bed that was covered in a fluffy white duvet. "Not as much a stranger as you think. Doesn't seem fair for me to know who you are when you don't know me." She held out her hand. "I'm Jess O'Malley," she said.

Amelia shook her hand. "It's nice to make your acquaintance, Mrs. O'Malley."

"Jess'll do." The woman's lips quirked. "I'm Quinn's sister," she added meaningfully.

Amelia's mouth went dry. "Oh."

Jess shifted and pulled a fancy phone from her back pocket, tapped on the screen a few times then held it out.

Amelia warily took the phone.

The sight of herself in Quinn's arms on the display didn't come as a shock. Since her supposed engagement, she'd become almost numb to the existence of such photographs. The fact that she'd drawn Quinn into the mess, though, caused a wave of grief. "Where'd you find this?"

"It's all over the internet."

She scrolled through the image then handed back the phone. Her mouth felt dry. "Has he seen it?"

"My brother? Or your fiancé?"

Amelia tucked her tongue behind her teeth, gathering her wits. Jess pulled as few punches as her brother. "Quinn."

"He's seen it." Jess sat forward, her arms on her knees. Her eyes—hazel, just like Quinn's, Amelia realized—were assessing. "He doesn't need his heart broken again, Lady Chesterfield. Once was bad enough."

"Amelia," she said faintly. She loathed the courtesy title of "Lady" when she hadn't done a single thing to earn it. "I'm not trying to break anyone's heart. Quinn—" She swallowed and looked away from his sister's eyes. "Your brother hates me, anyway."

"Hate and love are two sides of the same coin, hon."

"Not this time." One corner of her mind wondered if she'd have been better off facing Ophelia than Quinn's sister. And another corner of her mind argued that she would probably get her chance momentarily, because she had significant doubts that any teenager would be able to hold up under the determined paparazzo, no matter how devoted she was to her high school English teacher.

The rest of her mind was consumed with Quinn.

It didn't take a genius to know it was Quinn's ex-wife who'd caused his heartbreak. She pressed her numb lips together for a moment but her need overcame discretion. "What exactly did his ex-wife do to him?"

"Cheated on him with her ex-boyfriend." Jess's voice was flat and immediate. She clearly had no reservations about sharing the details. "Got pregnant and left him for her ex-boyfriend."

Amelia felt the blood drain out of her head. She sat very still, listening as Jess went on, oblivious to Amelia's shock.

"They're still married, living right here in Vicker's Corners. Didn't even have the decency to get out of Horseback Hollow's backyard." Her tone made it plain what she thought of that.

"I haven't cheated on anyone," Amelia said. Her voice sounded faraway. "Least of all Quinn." No matter what he believed right now, six weeks ago, she had been nothing but honest with him. As for James, she'd never made any promises to him either before or after her night with Quinn. And when she'd returned to all the engagement commotion, she'd told him about the man she'd met in Horseback Hollow. The man she'd intended on returning to.

Only that man had said in no uncertain terms that her return was no longer wanted at all.

How would Quinn react once she informed him of her pregnancy?

Trying not to cry, she stood and looked out the window again. There were a few vehicles driving up and down the street. A young family pushing a stroller was walking along the sidewalk, looking in the shop windows. The cars on either side of her aunt's in front of the post office had been replaced by different ones. The fire engine siren had gone quiet.

Ophelia hadn't come pounding up the stairs, her camera whirring away.

"D'you mind if I ask what you're doing in Texas?"

Amelia laughed silently and without humor. Learning she was pregnant had changed everything. She could no longer remain in England actually considering marriage to a man she didn't love. Regardless of what Jess had revealed about Quinn's ex-wife, he still needed to know he was going to be a father. And she had to learn how to become a mother.

She blinked hard several times before looking at Jess, more or less dry-eyed. "Yes." Even that one word sounded thick.

Jess's eyes narrowed for a moment. Then she smiled faintly. "Well, at least that's honest."

Amelia's eyes stung all over again. She looked away. "I'm not a Jezebel."

"No." Jess sighed audibly. "I want to say you're a twenty-three-old kid. But that'd be ironic coming from me since Mac and I already had two babies by the time I was your age." She rose also. "Stay here. I'll see if your nosy gal-pal is still snooping around downstairs."

Amelia waited tensely until Quinn's sister returned. "Shayla says she doesn't know you're up here, but she checked in to the room downstairs anyway," she said. "Unfortunately, that room opens right onto the lobby. And there's no convenient fire exit this time."

Dismayed, Amelia could do nothing but stare.

"Yeah." Jess rubbed her hands down the sides of her cutoff denims. "I didn't expect her to check in, either," she grumbled.

"What am I going to do?" Amelia stared at the room around them. "I can't stay here! I have to get my aunt's car back to her."

Jess patted her hands in the air, obviously trying to calm her. "I'll figure something out." She made a face. "Shayla couldn't very well turn down a paying customer. There are only three rooms here. But she said she'd try to let you know if your fan heads out to look for you. If not, just be glad there's an entire floor between you with a newlywed couple expected to occupy it." She gave her a wry smile. "Maybe they'll make enough noise you can sneak out without anyone noticing."

Try as she might, Amelia couldn't prevent heat from rising in her cheeks.

"Wow." Jess eyed her flush openly. "Just how sheltered *were* you growing up?"

Amelia blushed even harder. She thought of the private schools. The tutors. The chaperones. There were days when she and Lucie had felt like the only thing they were being raised for was to become a pristinely suitable choice for a noble marriage. Something their mother had vehemently denied since *her* first marriage had been just that type. Arranged. And terribly unhappy despite the production of Amelia's half brothers, Oliver and Brodie.

Jess looked at the sturdy watch on her wrist and made a face. "I'm going to have to leave you here. Just for a bit," she assured quickly. "I've got to pick up my two oldest from baseball and drop off my middle at karate class. But I'll be back in an hour, tops. And, I'll, uh, I'll make sure Shayla keeps quiet in the meantime. At least the room's comfortable and it has its own bathroom, right?"

Amelia wanted to chew off her tongue. "The room's comfortable," she allowed. But a prison was still a prison. "My aunt's car—"

"I promise. It's my fault you're stuck up here and I'll figure something out," Jess said again. "Just hang tight for a little bit. Here." She handed Amelia her cell phone. "I'll leave that with you to prove I'll be back quickly. Everyone knows I don't go far without my cell. Quinn's always complaining about it."

"Fine." Amelia took the phone only because Jess seemed so intent on it and once the other woman left, she set it on the narrow dresser against the wall across from the bed and went back to the window. She saw Jess hurry out from beneath the striped awning a few minutes later and heartily wished that it was Ophelia Malone who was the one departing.

It was warm in the room and she figured out how to open the window to let in some fresh air. Then she sat back down on the wicker rocker.

She didn't even realize she'd dozed off until the buzzing of Jess's phone startled her awake. She had no intentions of answering the other woman's phone, and she ignored the ringing until it stopped. She used the bathroom and turned on the small television sitting on one corner of the dresser and flipped through the meager selection. Black-and-white movies, a sitcom repeat and an obviously local talk show. She smiled a little when the hostess with a helmet of gray hair talked about the buzz surrounding the Horseback Hollow Cantina slated to open in two weeks, and switched the telly off again just as Jess's phone began ringing again.

She picked it up, hoping to find some way of silencing it. But the sight of Quinn's name bobbing on the phone's display stopped her. Her thumb hovered over the screen almost, *almost,* touching it.

But she sighed and turned the phone facedown on the dresser instead. The ringing immediately stopped and she went back to stare out the open window. The street outside was undeniably picturesque with its streetlights shaped like old-fashioned gas lamps and big pots of summer flowers hanging from them. Her aunt's car was now the only one in front of the post office. Everything looked peaceful and lovely and on any other day, she'd be perfectly charmed by the town.

When there was a bold knock on the door, she went rigid, feeling panicked all over again.

She wouldn't put it past Ophelia Malone to go door-to-door looking for her. She looked out the window. There was plenty of space for her to climb out, but nothing to climb onto. No terrace. No fire escape ladder. Just the awning below her window that hung over the front entrance.

She'd never jumped out of a window onto an awning but she'd jumped out of plenty of trees. Now she was pregnant, though, so that option was out no matter *how* badly she wanted to avoid the reporter.

The knock came again. Followed by a deep voice that she would recognize anywhere. "Open up, princess."

Not Ophelia.

Shaking more than ever, she ran to the door and pulled it open, looking up at Quinn for only a second before dragging him inside. "Are you *crazy?* What if someone saw you?"

He was wearing faded blue jeans that hugged his powerful thighs, a plain white T-shirt stretched over his broad shoulders and he needed a shave. Badly. And even though his lips were thin as he looked down at her, he still made her knees feel weak. "If answering a phone wasn't beneath your dignity, you wouldn't have missed an opportunity to get out of here."

"What?"

"Your camera-toting friend went to the sandwich shop next door."

"How do you even know what she looks like? I didn't see her leave." She reached around him for the door. "If we're quick—"

"She's already back," he cut her hopefulness short. "And there aren't a lot of people browsing around Vicker's Corners with that sort of camera clenched in their hands."

"Shayla was supposed to let me know if Ophelia left!"

"Yeah, well, Shayla's a seventeen-year-old kid and her mom sent her out on an errand."

"How do you know that?"

His expression turned even darker. He crossed to the window and glanced out. "Because I heard them when I came in to see why the hell you weren't answering the damn phone."

Her head swam and she leaned back against the door for support.

He crossed to the window and glanced out. "Jess called me from the park where her boys play baseball. She got tied up there with the coach trying to keep the guy from kicking Jason off the team for fighting. For some unfathomable reason she was worried about you."

She winced. "You can return her phone to her, then." She'd have to take her chances with Ophelia whether the prospect nauseated her or not.

She was a grown woman carrying a baby. She shouldn't need rescuing. Maybe that was one of the ways she was supposed to start acting like one. "You might have gotten up here without Ophelia seeing you, but try not to be caught on camera when you leave again." She reached behind her and closed her hand over the door-knob. "I appreciate your…efforts…but I need to get my aunt's car back to her. I'm sure the baby shower she's attending is over by now."

He looked impatient. "Jess told me about the car. I al-ready got hold of Deke. He's got Jeanne covered."

Amelia exhaled. At least that was something, though it didn't alleviate her anxiety over Ophelia, much less Quinn. "That was—" *unexpected* "—very good of you."

"Jess also told me she's the reason you're stuck here."

"*Ophelia*'s the reason. I never imagined that woman would go to these lengths for a few pictures to sell." Her stomach churned and her palm grew sweaty on the door-knob. "Regardless, you shouldn't have come."

"Afraid your fiancé'll find out?"

She strongly considered opening the door and walking out. Only the fact that she'd brought this on herself by not addressing the press—the legitimate press—straight-on from the beginning kept her from doing so.

She took her hand away from the doorknob and wiped it down the side of her borrowed sundress. "Insult me all you want. I still don't want Ophelia taking after you, too. Right now—" her lips twisted "—assuming she doesn't find us here *together,* all you are is a faceless man with dark hair. She's still focusing on me, and it's best to keep it that way."

"You'd prefer hiding out here on your own until she gives up and goes away?"

"If I confront her, she'll somehow use that for her own gain. I know how these people work, Quinn. She's not breaking any laws—"

"Yet. Or have you forgotten already about the ones who did when they hacked into your phone calls?"

She sighed. She would never forget. "Ophelia doesn't know for certain that I'm here. And she can't stay cooped up in this B and B forever. She's not gaining anything unless she has photos to sell."

Or a story.

And Amelia's pregnancy would be a whale of a tale. It would put the detestable woman's career on the map, at least until the next scandal came along.

"I'm just grateful your sister happened to be in the hardware store at the right time to provide a distraction." It was at least one thing that had gone her way.

His lips curled derisively. "Don't kid yourself, princess. My sister never *happens* to do anything."

"She was there to buy pink paint for her daughter's room!"

"Jess doesn't *have* a daughter. And I can promise you that none of my nephews would be caught dead in a pink room."

"But—"

"Don't try to figure it out," he suggested darkly. He paced around the room as if he found it as cagelike as she. "Jess is a law unto herself. She's just as infected with royal-fever as the rest of the people around here."

Except for him. He'd been fully vaccinated, courtesy of an engagement that didn't exist.

"I don't care why she was there," Amelia said abruptly. "Facing your sister, whatever her reasons, is always going to be preferable to Ophelia Malone. At least she's—" She broke off.

"At least she's what?"

Family. Amelia stared at him, the word she'd been about to blurt still alarmingly close to her lips.

Just tell him.

She'd wanted a chance to speak with him alone, and now she had it.

Just tell him!

Her mouth ran dry. She started to speak. "O-only trying to protect you," she finished, instead.

His eyes narrowed, studying her face so closely she had to work hard not to squirm.

"I wish I had another disguise," she said. "We could just get out of here. Even if Ophelia doesn't discover us, Shayla's mother probably will."

"We don't have to worry about her." He pulled something from his pocket and tossed it on the bed.

She eyed the old-fashioned key.

"I rented the room for the night," he added flatly.

Amelia's stomach hollowed out. "We're *both* stuck here?"

Chapter Seven

Quinn paced across the room, putting as much distance as he could between them. "I'm not the one who's stuck," he corrected.

The bed with the puffy white comforter loomed large between them. Particularly when she sank down on the corner of the mattress.

With the red dress and her dark, dark hair, she looked like she might have been posed there for an advertisement. If not for the fact that her face was nearly as white as the bedding.

He ruthlessly squashed down his concern.

"I can come and go any time I want," he continued. "You're the one who isn't supposed to be here."

"Right. Silly of me to forget," she murmured.

He exhaled roughly. "Maybe she'll want to go out for dinner later and we'll be able to get out of here."

Before morning.

Before they spent an entire night together in a room with only one freaking bed.

He pinched the bridge of his nose and sat on the rocking chair. The wicker creaked a little under his weight, sounding loud in the quiet room.

He cleared his throat. "How many times have you had to do this?"

"Hide out from paparazzi?" She pushed her hair behind her ear. "I have no idea. Lucie and I've been doing it since we were teenagers, I guess."

Lucie, he knew, was her older sister. "She doesn't seem to be in the news as much as you."

"That's just because nobody thinks she's marrying a future earl right now. We've always been in a fishbowl, but never as bad as the last several weeks have been." She rubbed her hands nervously over the bed beside her hips.

He looked away. Whether she looked terrifyingly fragile or not, imagining her hair spread out over all that white was way too easy and the effect it was having on him wasn't one he needed just then. "It's a first for me," he muttered.

She spread her hands, smiling without any real amusement. "Welcome to my world." Then even the fake smile died. "You didn't tell me before—" Her lashes swept down. "In April I mean, that you were married."

It was the last thing he expected to hear and as a cold shower, it was pretty effective.

"It was a long time ago," he finally said.

"How long?"

"Why does it matter?"

"Because you're painting me to be just like her."

His jaw tightened. Knowing she was right didn't mean that he was wrong. "History tends to repeat itself."

Her long throat worked. "You have no idea," she murmured.

The hairs on the back of his neck stood up and he sat forward. The chair creaked ominously. "What's *that* supposed to mean?"

She pushed off the bed and pressed her hands together. "Look, despite you trying to help me here, I understand that things are…are over between us. You've been more than clear about that. And no matter what I say I don't expect that to change. You are not under any obligation—"

His jaw tightened. "Amelia—"

She moistened her lips. Her dark brown eyes met his, then flicked away again. Her tension was palpable.

"I'm pregnant," she said in a low voice. "I came back to Horseback Hollow to tell you."

He stared at her. There was a strange, hollow ringing inside his head. "You're…pregnant."

She chewed her lip. "Keep your voice down. Who knows how thin the walls are."

"You're *pregnant*," he repeated, a little more softly, but no less incredulously.

"And saying it a third time won't change that fact." She went into the adjoining bathroom and returned with a glass of water. She pushed it into his hand. "Drink."

The kind of drink he felt in sudden need of came out of a bottle and was strong enough to put down a horse. He set the glass on the windowsill. "How do you know?"

She paced across the room again. "The usual way."

"You missed your period?"

A tinge of color finally lit her cheeks. She didn't look at him. "Yes."

"And you're saying its mine."

"Yes." The word grew clipped.

"Even though you're engaged to someone else."

She thrust her fingers through her hair and tugged. "I am *not* engaged!" She dropped her hands and sank onto the foot of the bed again. "And before you accuse me, I know this baby is yours because you're the only man I've ever slept with," she added in a flat voice.

He shook his head once, sharp enough to clear it of the fog that had filled it. "You expect me to believe you were a virgin? And I didn't happen to notice?"

Her cheeks turned bright. "I don't care what you noticed or not. That night with you was the only time I—" She broke off. "This baby is not James's," she said crisply. "What earthly reason would I have for being here—" she lifted her arms "—if it were? You think I like facing you and, and telling you—" her voice grew choked "—knowing how you feel about me?"

"Calm down."

"Easy for you to say." She rushed into the bathroom and slammed the door behind her.

He sat there, hearing his pulse pounding in his head. Remembering that April night. The dawn following.

She'd been shy, yes. At first. But he'd never suspected—

He shoved to his feet, crossed the room and pushed open the door.

She was sitting on the closed lid of the commode, tears sliding down her cheeks. And her jaw dropped at his intrusion. "What—"

"It's only been six weeks." He bit out the fact that

she'd been so careful to point out to him. "How can you be certain? Do you have any other symptoms? Have you seen a doctor?"

Her expression went smooth, her eyes remote. "I did a home pregnancy test."

"Sometimes they come back false." He grimaced when she just looked at him. "Another experience from my regrettable marriage." Before the "I do's" Carrie's test had been positive. After, the test was negative. But he couldn't even accuse her of lying about it, because at that point, he'd still believed she loved him and he'd been right beside her when they'd looked at those test results.

Carrie had been relieved.

He hadn't been. Not at that point, anyway. He'd built their house with a family in mind. A family that had never come. Not for him.

"Two years later she got pregnant for real," he added abruptly.

"With her ex-boyfriend's child."

He studied her for a long moment but could see nothing in her expressionless eyes. "Either you've been listening to really old gossip or my sister's got a big mouth."

She didn't respond to that. "I'll agree to whatever tests you want." Her tone was still cool.

He really, really hated that "royal" face of hers. "Another pregnancy test will do for starters."

Her brows lifted, surprise evidently overcoming remoteness. "I meant paternity tests."

"I know." He could only deal with so much at once. "When you arrived in my barn, you were worn out. Exhausted and full of stress. You collapsed, for God's sake. Let's just make certain there's a pregnancy to begin with."

She sucked in her lower lip for a moment. "I don't think now's a good time for me to stroll into a pharmacy to buy a test kit."

He stifled an oath. For a moment there, he'd managed to forget the very reason they were in the guest room at all. "After we get back to the Hollow," he said. "My sister's pregnant so often she's probably got a stockpile of tests."

As far as humor went, it fell flatter than a pancake.

Turning slightly, she swiped her hand over her cheek. As if he couldn't see perfectly well that she was crying.

"First things first," he said gruffly. "Sooner or later, your stalker downstairs will have to eat. Or sleep. And then we'll get the hell out of this place."

"Here." Several hours later, Shayla handed Quinn a set of keys on a key chain with a plastic heart hanging from it. "Mrs. O'Malley said to give these to you, too."

It was finally dark and Ophelia had left the B and B, presumably for dinner, though Shayla reported that she'd had her camera with her when she'd gone.

The teenager—who clearly thought she was taking part in an exciting adventure—had also delivered a knapsack much like the one Amelia had ditched in the airport restroom, filled with clothing and a long blond wig.

"Those are the keys to Mrs. O'Malley's van?"

The girl nodded, looking conspiratorial. "It's parked at the end of the block in front of the bar. You could see it from your window if you looked out."

The bar, Amelia knew, was O'Malley's and it belonged to Jess's father-in-law. She looked at Quinn. Aside from working out their escape plan with his sister and Shayla, he hadn't said much in the past few hours.

He hadn't done much except watch Amelia, leaving her to imagine all manner of dark thoughts he was having about her.

"I can just as easily drive my aunt's car," she argued not for the first time.

"Ophelia probably already knows it belongs to your aunt," he returned, also not for the first time. "It's been sitting there all day even though the post office closed at noon."

As long as Ophelia didn't spot them together, there was no reason for him not to drive his own pickup truck back to Horseback Hollow.

Her stomach was churning. The longer they'd waited in the pretty guest suite, the crazier she'd felt. The news that Ophelia had left the B and B on foot had been a relief, but it didn't mean the end of her problems.

Not by any stretch of the imagination.

"I'll change into the clothes then." It wasn't as if she had many options. She looked at Shayla. "You've been a big help, Shayla."

The girl bounced on her toes. "Are you kidding? Nothing interesting ever happens here! I'm just glad my ma's out on a date tonight. I love her, but if she knew *you* were here, so would the rest of the town. She can't keep anything a secret." Holding her finger to her lips, she slipped out the door and closed it behind her.

Amelia exhaled and, avoiding Quinn's gaze, took the clothing into the bathroom. She changed into the diminutive bandage of a skirt that was as bright an orange as Shayla's hair and the white V-neck shirt that came with it. Amelia wasn't wearing a bra and when she pulled the thin cotton over her head, she cringed at her reflection. The neckline reached midway down her chest and the shadow from her nipples showed clearly through the fabric.

If she asked for another blouse, though, they'd be delayed even longer. And they had no idea how long a window Ophelia was unwittingly allowing them. So she swallowed her misgivings and wound her hair into a knot on her head before pulling on the cheap wig that Shayla had provided. The hair was synthetic and an obviously false platinum blond. But it covered Amelia's dark hair and reached down to her waist.

As a disguise, she decided she far preferred the boy look she and Molly had attempted.

She kept the sandals on that she was already wearing. There was nothing distinctive about them and the platform wedges that Shayla had stuck in the knapsack were too small anyway. Then she zipped the discarded dress inside the pack and, hauling in a steadying breath, opened the door to face Quinn.

"Jesus," he muttered.

"I look like a tart," she said before he could.

"You look like jail bait." His gaze was focused on her chest.

Flushing, she dragged the cheap blond hair over her shoulders so it covered her breasts. "Are you ready to leave or not?"

In answer, he opened the door and handed her the heart-shaped key ring. "Like we agreed. You first. I'll follow in a few minutes. We'll meet up at the Rocking-U. You remember how to get there?"

"I got there on foot. I imagine I can get there by van." Squeezing the hard metal heart in her fist, she left the room.

This wasn't her first rodeo, as they said, when it came

to avoiding the paparazzi, but it was the first time she'd done so as a scantily clad teenage girl. Even when she'd *been* a teen, she'd never dressed like this. Her parents wouldn't have allowed it.

She encountered no one on the stairs between the third and second floors. On the second, she could hear music coming from behind the door of the honeymooners who had arrived a short while ago. On the last flight, she descended more gingerly.

But Shayla, dusting again though there was surely no need for it, caught her eye and quickly nodded. "All clear, Lady Amelia," she whispered loudly.

Resisting the urge to look back up the staircase to see if Quinn was watching, Amelia skipped down the rest of the stairs and sailed across the small lobby and out into the night air. She turned left, walking briskly to the end of the block, waiting with every footstep to hear a camera shutter clicking or see a camera flash lighting the night.

But there was nothing.

And soon she was jogging. Then running flat out, the knapsack bouncing wildly against her backside, until she reached the green van right where it was supposed to be. Her heart was pounding in her chest as she fumbled with the keys, nearly dropping them, before managing to unlock the door and climb inside. Once there, she worked the knapsack free and tossed it behind the seat before fitting the key into the ignition.

The engine started immediately and she cautiously drove away from the curb. She hadn't been accustomed to her aunt's car and the van—considerably larger—felt even more unwieldy to her.

She drove around the corner, then the next and the next until she was right back where she'd begun the day, near the post office. She waited for a car to pass, then turned again and headed out of town. Back to Horse-back Hollow.

Going from one fire into the next.

Amelia was sitting at Quinn's piano, rubbing her fingers over the keys but not really playing anything, when he arrived. He walked over to the piano and deliberately closed the lid on the keys as if he couldn't stand the idea of her touching it.

"Here." He tossed her a small white sack. "I stopped at the drugstore on the way back."

She dumped out the contents on her lap.

A three-pack of pregnancy test kits.

Evidently, he *really* wanted to be certain.

"Decide you didn't want to let your sister know?"

His smile was thin. "Something like that."

She dropped the paper sack on top of the discarded blond wig sitting on top of the piano and turned the box over, pretending to read the instructions on the back, but not seeing any of the words.

She'd been waiting nearly an hour alone at his home before he got there. He'd told her the door wouldn't be locked, and it hadn't been. Only the fact that she needed the loo had made her go in, though.

Otherwise, she would have just sat in his sister's van and waited.

It wasn't as if he truly wanted her in his home, after all.

"You weren't followed?"

He shook his head once.

She pressed her lips together and rose. "I suppose you want me to do this now?" She waved the box slightly.

"You want to wait until morning?"

She wanted to turn back the calendar six weeks and do things right. She wanted the warm, tender man back that he'd been the night they'd made love.

Her eyes burned. Not answering, she walked past him and down the hall to the bathroom there. When she was finished, she put the cap back on the stick and left it sitting on the bathroom counter.

She opened the door to find him standing on the other side and heat ran up under her cheeks. "Two minutes."

He lifted his hand and she realized he was holding a pocket watch.

"My father used to carry a pocket watch," she murmured.

He crossed his arms and leaned back against the bathroom door, his hooded gaze on the test stick. "So did mine. This one." He dangled the watch from the chain. "One of the few things the fire didn't take. This and the piano." He could have been discussing the weather for all the emotion in his voice.

She chewed the inside of her lip.

Never had two minutes passed so slowly.

When finally it had, he picked up the stick and studied it silently. Then he flipped it into the little trash can next to the cabinet.

"It's late," he said, walking past her. "You need to eat."

Amelia's throat tightened.

Even though she knew, she *knew* what the test would show, she plucked the plastic stick out of the empty can and looked at the bright blue plus sign.

Tears slid out of her eyes and she dropped it in the trash once more.

She turned on the cold water and splashed it over her

face until her cheeks felt frozen. Then she dried her face and followed him.

He was in the kitchen. Just as he had been the night he'd found her in his barn.

Only this time the sandwich was sitting on a plate, and a glass of milk sat next to that.

Her stomach lurched. Whether from a sudden attack of morning sickness-at-night or from the horrible day it had been she didn't know. But the thought of choking down any kind of food just then made her want to retch.

She forced herself to sit down, though, in front of the plate. He, however, remained standing by the window, looking out into the night. "Aren't you going to eat?" He had spent nearly as much time cooped up in the B and B as she had.

"We'll go to the justice of the peace on Monday." He didn't look at her. "Unless you want a minister. It'll be more complicated that way, but—"

"A *minister*." She pushed aside the plate and stared at his back. "What are you suggesting?"

He turned, giving her a narrow look. "What do you think? My kid's not going to be born without my name."

Her jaw went loose. "So," she said with false cheer, "now you magically believe it's yours?"

His lips twisted. "Don't push me, princess."

She shoved back from the table so abruptly the chair tipped over and crashed to the tiled floor. "Don't push *you*? I can't believe I ever thought I—" She broke off, grasping for some semblance of self-control even though she wanted to launch herself at him, kicking and screaming. Which was altogether shocking, because she never lost her temper like that. "If I wanted a marriage without love, I could have stayed in England and married Jimmy! It certainly would have been easier than this!"

"That—" he pointed toward her midsection "—changes things."

She lifted her chin, channeling her mother at her most regal. "It doesn't change the fact that I won't be arranged into a convenient marriage. I've done a lot of things in my life purely for propriety's sake, but not this."

He swore and planted his boot on one leg of the up-turned chair and kicked it away from her.

She gasped as it slammed against the wall.

"Next time you give me that royal face, I'll put you over my knee." He leaned over her, tall and furious. "And I won't let you take *my kid* back there to be raised by another man!"

Shocked to her very core, she stood there frozen. "I wouldn't do that."

A muscle ticked angrily in his jaw and his eyes raked over her face.

"I swear to you, Quinn." She stared into his eyes, wishing with all of her heart that he'd just take her in his arms the way he had six weeks ago. "I would never do that," she finished hoarsely.

"Then you can prove it on Monday in front of the JP."

She hauled in an unsteady breath. Marriage to Quinn Drummond was something she'd dreamed about since they'd made love. Since they'd unknowingly created the baby inside her.

But not this way.

Not ever this way.

"No."

Then she retrieved the chair, turned it upright and tucked it under the table and walked out of the kitchen.

Chapter Eight

When he heard the front door open and close, Quinn bolted after her, catching her at the bottom of the porch steps. "Where the *hell* do you think you're going?"

She yanked her arm out of his grasp and gave him a glacial look. "Where I go is not *up* to you."

"You wanna strut out to the highway and hitch a ride, princess?" His lips twisted as he looked her over. "Imagine a trucker will go by eventually. Depending on what sort of guy he is, he might or might not stop for someone looking like you."

She gave a futile yank down on the hem of the skirt that showed nearly every inch of her gloriously God-given stems. "You are *not* the man I thought you were," she said through her teeth.

"And you aren't the woman I thought, either," he returned.

She turned on the heel of her little sandals, her hair flying around her shoulders and started walking away, her sweet hips swaying.

He cussed like he hadn't cussed since he was fifteen and his mom had washed out his mouth with soap. "You're not going anywhere, princess." In two long steps, he reached her and hooked her around the waist, swinging her off her feet before she had a chance to stop him.

Her legs scissored and he slid her over his shoulder, clamping his arm over the back of her legs before she could do either one of them physical damage. "Cut it out."

She drummed her fists against his backside, trying to wriggle out of his hold. "Put me *down* this instant," she ordered imperiously.

"I warned you," he said and swatted her butt.

She pounded his back even harder. "You...cretin."

"Yeah, yeah. Sweet nothings won't get you anywhere, princess." He stomped back into the house and into the living room. He lifted her off his shoulder and dumped her on the sofa.

She bounced and tried scrambling away, but he leaned over her, pinning her on either side with his hands. "Stay," he bit out.

She glared at him through the hair hanging in her face. "I. Don't. Take. Orders." Her chest heaved.

He didn't move.

Didn't do a damn thing even though he should have, because she was there, in his house and she was pregnant with his kid and he didn't want to ask for a polite dance or gentle, moonlit kisses.

He just *wanted*.

With a need that was blinding.

She suddenly went still.

A swallow worked down her long, long throat and the glint in her eyes shifted to something else entirely.

She moistened her lips. "Quinn," she whispered.

And then her hands weren't pushing at him, they were pulling.

At his shirt that he ripped off over his head.

At his belt that slid out of his belt loops with a loud slither.

"Hurry," she gasped, squirming beneath him as she yanked his fly apart and dragged at his jeans, nearly sending his nerves out the top of his skull.

He reached under that excuse of a skirt and tore her panties aside. She was wet and hot and she gasped when he dragged her closer and drove into her.

He let out a harsh breath, trying to slow down, get some control, get some sanity, but she wrapped her lithe legs around his hips, greedily rocking. And then she was shuddering deep, deep inside, her body clutching at him and her lips crying out his name.

And he was lost.

Every cell Amelia possessed was still vibrating when Quinn silently rolled away. She felt like they'd just been tossed out of a tornado.

The night they'd made love had been magical. Tender. Sweet.

This was…raw. Most assuredly not sweet.

And every bit as powerful.

She let out a shuddering breath, knowing that if he touched her again, she'd welcome him just as wantonly. "Quinn—"

"This shouldn't have happened." He sat up and slid

off the sofa. He didn't look at her as he fastened his jeans and his voice was low. "Did I hurt you?"

She caught her breath, aching inside. "No," she whispered honestly. "Did…did I hurt you?" She dimly recalled her nails sinking into his flesh while pleasure exploded inside her.

He looked over his shoulder at that, genuinely surprised. His gaze raked over her and she trembled, muscles deep inside her still clenching. The thin cotton shirt felt rough against her agonizingly tight nipples and she tugged the skirt down where it belonged. She had no idea what had become of her underpants.

"No," he said gruffly. "You didn't hurt me." He leaned over and picked up his T-shirt. The neckline was nearly torn right out of it. He looked at it for a moment, then bunched it in his fist. "I'll get you something to put on."

She sat up, curling her legs to the side. "Thank you."

The roping muscles defining his strong shoulders seemed to tighten when she spoke. He went up the stairs and returned in minutes with a button-down shirt. "You still need to eat," he said evenly, handing it to her. "And decide if you want a minister or not."

Then he turned and went into the kitchen. Through the doorway she could see him readjusting the chair.

Her eyes stung.

She didn't know what she was going to do.

But she knew she was not going to marry Quinn Drummond without his love.

Swiping her cheeks, she stood on legs that felt as insubstantial as candy floss. The shirt he'd given her was clearly a dress shirt but it definitely wasn't the one he'd worn to Toby's wedding. That one had been stark white while this one was a pale gray with an even paler pinstripe. When she unbuttoned it and found a tag still attached to the collar inside, she realized it was new. Never been worn.

She'd have preferred something he'd worn. At least she'd have been able to take a little comfort from it. And she wouldn't be wondering who'd bought the shirt for him because it looked too fancy for anything he'd have chosen for himself.

She removed the tag and pulled the shirt over the one she already had on. New or not, there was something very intimate about wearing his shirt. She needed all the barriers against that feeling that she could get.

She buttoned it up, then folded the long sleeves over several times until they didn't hang past her wrists. She spotted her panties and picked them up. The thin silk was torn in two.

Thank goodness the shirttails reached her knees, though just thinking why that was a good thing made her cheeks hot and her stomach hollow out.

She toed off the one sandal that she was still wearing, blushed some more over that as well, then hurried down the hall to the bathroom, the ruined silk bunched in her fist.

She washed up, dropped the panties in the trash next to the test stick, and tried to restore some order to her tangled hair with her fingers. Finally, with no other excuses remaining, she returned to the kitchen.

The sandwich was still there on the plate.

He was sitting in the chair opposite it, his long legs stretched out across the floor, a dark brown bottle propped on his hard, tanned abdomen.

She ignored the curling sensation inside her belly at the sight and sat down. Unlike earlier, she was suddenly famished, but she cringed a little when she picked up the sandwich, because the bread hadn't even had an opportunity to grow stale while they'd been…been—

"Don't think about it," he said abruptly and she jumped a little.

"I beg your pardon?"

"You're thinking about what we just did on the couch." His hazel eyes were hooded and unreadable. "My suggestion is don't." He lifted the bottle to his lips and took a long drink. "Safer that way," he added when he set the bottle down again. The glass clinked a little when it hit the metal tab still unfastened at the top of his jeans.

She dragged her eyes away and took a bite of the sandwich. For something that had transpired in a span of minutes, she was quite certain *not* thinking about it wasn't going to be as easy as he made it out to be.

"I didn't have anything but peanut butter and jelly," he said.

She chewed and swallowed. "I like peanut butter."

His lips twisted a little. "So do my nephews. They go through a jar every time they're here."

She gingerly took a sip of milk. On a good day, she didn't much care for it, and now was no exception. She slid out of the chair and saw his eyes narrow. "I prefer water," she said quickly, lifting the glass. She dumped the milk down the drain, rinsed the glass and refilled it from the tap then sat down again to the sandwich. "Your sister really doesn't have a daughter?"

"She really doesn't," he said evenly.

"How old are her boys?"

"Fifteen, thirteen, nine, six and two."

"Goodness." She toyed with the water glass. He might not have told her before about an ex-wife, but he had

talked about his family. The death of his father. The fact
that he had only one older sister.

"Who else knows you're pregnant?"

She looked at him quickly, then back at the sandwich.
"Just, um, just Molly." She tore off a tiny piece of crust.
"She's one of my mother's secretaries."

He bent his knees and shifted forward, setting the
bottle on the table. "You told a *secretary?* Not a friend
or your sister?"

"Molly is a friend. And Lucie—" She shook her head.
"Lucie's busy with her own issues. Besides, we've never
exactly shared secrets."

"Thought you were close in age?"

"We are. She's only two years ahead. But—" She
shrugged. "We've all had our responsibilities growing
up. Some more than others." She smashed the tidbit of
crust between her thumbs. "Mostly, mine has been to
provide window dressing at my mother's events."

"You pulled together the companies who funded that
last orphanage. That's a little more than window dressing."

She looked at him and it was his turn to glance away
and shrug. "I can read," he muttered. "And Jess was
yammering on about it not too long ago."

In other words, don't get excited thinking he'd been
following her activities. She wondered how impressed
he'd be if he knew the companies she'd been able to pull
together for the funding were all controlled by the Earl
of Estingwood, and took another bite of the sandwich.

The peanut butter and jelly stuck to the roof of her
mouth, reminding her of the sandwiches she used to
beg off their cook when she was a little girl. "Well—"
she swallowed it down with another drink of water
"—speaking of reading. We might have avoided Oph-

elia Malone for now, but I doubt she'll go quietly into the night."

"She got lucky with one photo," he dismissed.

"Sometimes one photo is all it takes to set off a firestorm."

"Afraid your—" he hesitated for a moment "—future earl is going to see it?"

She was certain he'd been going to say *fiancé*. Undoubtedly, James and his staff had already seen the photo and were organizing the appropriate damage control. But she didn't share that fact because Quinn wouldn't want to hear about it. "May I use your phone?" she asked instead.

He looked at the pocket watch he'd left earlier on the table. "Nearly eleven. Your aunt figures we're still in Vicker's Corners."

"I'm not calling my aunt." It would be early in London, but James always rose early. "I'm calling James."

His hazel eyes went flat. "Missing Lord Banning already?"

"If I didn't know better, I'd think you were jealous," she said sweetly. Of course he wasn't. He'd have to feel something other than reluctant lust and duty for him to be jealous. "May I use your phone or not?"

He picked up his bottle and gestured with the bottom of it. "It's right there on the wall, princess."

And he wasn't inclined to give her any privacy. That was more than apparent.

She went over to the phone that was, indeed, hanging on the wall just inside the doorway. Even though she knew Quinn had built the house within the past ten years, the phone was an old-fashioned thing with a long coiled cord tethering the receiver to the base. She plucked the receiver off the hook and punched out the numbers she knew by heart. After a number of clicks and burps, the line finally connected and James answered.

"It's Amelia," she greeted. She could feel Quinn's eyes boring holes in her backside. "How's your father?"

"Amelia! Where the bloody hell have you been? The media here is going mad. Not even your mother knew you were leaving. Are you all right?"

"I know. And I…I'm fine." She absently worked her finger into the center of the coiling phone cord. "You've got to issue a statement that we're not being married."

Even across the continents, she could hear his sigh. "You're back with that fellow, then."

She didn't know how she'd describe the situation with Quinn, but "back with" wouldn't be it. "I know what you'd hoped, Jimmy, but you've got to trust me. It's better to come from you. And the sooner the better." She looked over her shoulder when she heard a scrape on the floor.

Quinn had pushed back his chair and he walked past her, leaving the room.

"Ophelia's been hunting me around," she said into the phone, wanting to laugh a little hysterically because there was a gun rack containing several rifles attached to the wall above the doorway.

"If you hadn't given her something to find, she'd have had to give up," James returned. "You let her catch you kissing that man."

She exhaled, pressing her forehead to the cream-colored wall for a moment. "Just tell your father the truth," she said. "Tell him you're not in love with me. You never were!"

"Father doesn't care about love. He cares about bloodlines and he decided a year ago that yours was the right one."

"A marriage between us would be a disaster." She said the same thing she'd been telling him for months, ever since the whole idea of a union between them had come up. "You're in love with Astrid and I'm—"

"In love with your Horseback Hollow rancher," he finished and sighed again. "Father's condition is worse. He's home still. Refuses to go to hospital. Says there's no point alerting the vultures and he wants to die in his own bed."

She exhaled. "I'm so sorry, Jimmy." For all the earl's faults, he thought he knew what was best for his son. "How's your mum?"

"A rock, like always. Can you just hold on a few more days, Amelia? That's what the doctors have told us he has left. Days." He cleared his throat. "Once father is… gone…I'll issue a statement. You won't come out looking badly. I'll blame it on my increased duties or something. Mutual decision and all that."

She knew his request wasn't because of the Earldom he'd inherit. It was because, despite the problems between them, he wanted his father to die in peace, believing his son was on the track he'd laid.

"A few days," she agreed huskily.

"Thank you. You've been a good friend, Amelia." She heard him speaking to someone in muffled tones, then he came back. "I have to go. Take care of yourself. And look out for Ophelia Malone."

"I will." The line clicked, going dead and she unwound her fingers from the cord and replaced the receiver. She left the kitchen, thinking that Quinn would be in the living area. But he wasn't. Nor was he upstairs.

She went to the window and pulled up the blinds, looking out. She could see a light on inside the barn and she pushed her feet back into the sandals and went outside. The night air was balmy and quite a bit warmer than it had been six weeks earlier, and it smelled earthy and green.

He'd parked his pickup truck next to where she'd left his sister's van and she walked around them as she headed toward the barn. Unlike the house, which he'd built not so long ago, the barn looked like it had stood there for generations and in the dark now, with gold light spewing out the opened doorway, it looked almost medieval. She stepped inside.

Quinn, still shirtless, was stacking bales of hay against one wall.

She pulled in a soundless breath at the sight of him, entirely too aware of her lack of undergarments beneath the shirttails.

Her sandals scuffed the hard packed ground and he looked at her.

"I, um, I would have been much less nervous the other night had I known there were lights in here," she said, gesturing with her hand toward the row of industrial looking fixtures hanging high overhead.

He turned his back and tossed another bale into place. She wasn't sure why. To her, it looked as if he were just moving the stack from one spot to another.

She rubbed her damp palms down her thighs. "James will issue a statement in a few days."

He just kept working. "Why the wait?"

She hesitated and saw the way his lips twisted as if she'd done exactly what he expected.

Annoyed, she walked across the barn, feeling bits of straw and grit crunching beneath her shoes. "I told you James's father is in poor health. He's also been hiding that fact because, in addition to being the Earl of Estingwood, he is head of Estingwood Mills."

"The textiles."

She wondered if he'd learned that courtesy of his sister, or if he'd found out on his own. "James has been running the company in his father's stead and fending off a takeover bid by one of their competitors. If the earl's health was made public it would endanger their hold. Once James succeeds his father, that will no longer be the case. The mill will be safe, as will the hundreds of people it employs."

"Again, why the wait?" His tone was hard.

"The title is passed on at the earl's discretion during his lifetime, or to his son upon his death which, according to James, sadly is fairly imminent. Before now, he's insisted that James be married to an appropriate mate before receiving the title and had been doing his best to see that happened."

He tossed another hay bale and turned to her. "So the old man was yanking Banning's strings."

"I suppose it might look that way." Sweat gleamed across his broad chest and she looked away, shocked at how badly she wanted to press her mouth against that salty sheen. "Lord Banning's not a bad man. He just has very traditional expectations where his family is concerned. You behave suitably. You marry suitably."

"Fine. The old man kicks the bucket in a few days. So which is it going to be? Justice of the peace or a minister?"

Stymied, she just stared. "Your callousness aside, regardless of what announcements James makes, I'm still not marrying you like this!"

He tugged off the worn leather gloves he'd been wearing and grabbed the shotgun she hadn't even noticed leaning against the wall.

"I've heard of shotgun weddings," she said, smiling weakly, "but this is taking it too literally."

"I've got a possum."

She blinked. "Excuse me?"

"A possum," he repeated with exaggerated care. "It's raiding my feed."

She grimaced. "And you want to shoot it?"

"I don't want to make it a pet," he drawled. "Ranching, princess." He dragged the leather gloves beneath her chin and flicked her hair behind her shoulder. "It's not fine linens and sidesaddles."

Fine linens had their place, but she was just as happy sitting in the kitchen with a peanut butter and jelly sandwich. "I've never once sat sidesaddle," she said with a cool smile. "Some of the Chesterfields are champion riders. I do know what manure smells like."

"You'll get even more familiar with it." He smiled, too, but it was fierce-looking and dangerous. "Along with the stench of branding and the mess of castrating. JP or minister?"

Her smile wilted. Her stomach lurched more alarmingly than ever before and she suddenly knew it wasn't going to go away so easily this time.

She whirled on her heel and barely made it outside of the barn before she leaned over and vomited right onto the dirt.

Quinn came up beside her.

"This is the most humiliating moment of my life," she managed miserably. "Please, *please* just leave me alone."

He carefully gathered her hair behind her shoulders. "Not a chance in hell, princess."

Chapter Nine

"There you are!" Jeanne Marie waved her hand from the window of her car and pulled up alongside Quinn's pickup truck. She got out quickly and strode across the gravel, a wide smile on her face.

Even though Amelia had gotten a few hours of actual sleep after tossing her cookies the night before, her stomach still felt rocky half a day later. She gingerly pushed out of the porch chair where she'd been sitting, soaking up the fresh afternoon air while Tanya, the teenager Quinn paid to clean his house, worked inside, and went down the three steps to greet her aunt. "I'm so sorry about the car."

"Oh." Jeanne Marie waved her hand. "These things happen." Then she laughed. "Well, not exactly *these* things. Nobody around here has ever had to hide out from the paparazzi before. But it turned out perfectly convenient for me. After church, Deke dropped me off in Vicker's Corners and was able to go back home rather than waiting around while I browsed the shops for you. Which made him a very happy camper." She gave Amelia a quick, squeezing hug. "And I'm glad that you didn't go to church this morning. That woman with the camera was there asking questions about you." She sniffed. "Not that *anyone* gave her the time of day."

"A fine churchlike attitude," Amelia said wryly, though she was glad the citizens of Horseback Hollow were showing some discretion, even if it was only because of loyalty to her aunt.

Jeanne Marie laughed again. "Now. Shall we discuss this *nothing* going on between you and Quinn?" She looked over Amelia's head at the ranch house behind her.

Amelia assumed her aunt didn't know about the internet photograph or she would have mentioned it. And she was glad for that. "Something is going on. I'm just—" she tugged at the red sundress that she'd pulled on yet again that morning "—not ready to say exactly what that is."

Her aunt's eyes narrowed a little, studying her. "At least you don't look quite like the whipped puppy that you did last week, so I'll give you a pass for now. Have you spoken with your mother?"

Amelia nodded. She'd called Josephine that morning and told her that the false engagement was over, though not the entire reason why. She wasn't ready to share her pregnancy with anyone other than Quinn, though she knew she'd need to sooner rather than later. She couldn't very well wait until she was round as a house. Her mum had been glad to hear about the pretense coming to an end, but Amelia wasn't so sure how she'd react to having another grandchild. Her brother Oliver had little Ollie already, but at least he'd been born *before* Oliver and his wife divorced.

Amelia could be married before her baby arrived, too, if she were willing to marry a man who didn't love her.

"She's really looking forward to coming for the Cantina's grand opening," Amelia told Jeanne Marie. "She hinted that she might be able to stay a few days longer than she expected."

"That would be marvelous." Jeanne turned back to her car and opened the back door. She pulled out a plastic shopping bag and handed it to Amelia. "Whatever doesn't fit can be returned," she said. "I made sure of that."

Amelia peeked inside the bag, seeing a couple T-shirts, a skirt and a package of white cotton underpants. "Perfect," she breathed. "Thank you so much, Aunt Jeanne." She carried the bag up onto the porch and set it on the wooden rocking chair and her aunt followed.

"Where's Quinn?"

"Off doing chores," she said vaguely. She wasn't entirely sure, because she'd been giving the man a wide berth since he'd insisted she take his bed the night before.

She'd been as wary of instigating another episode that led to torn panties as she was finding herself weakly admitting that she preferred a minister over a justice of the peace.

And her cheeks heated just thinking of panties and a minister in the same thought.

She realized her aunt was watching her thoughtfully, and quickly plucked the receipt for the purchases out of the bag. She drew a couple folded bills to cover the amount out of her sundress pocket and handed them to her aunt.

"All right now," Jeanne Marie said, tucking the cash in her own pocket. "Can you and Quinn come for dinner later? Christopher and his gal, Kinsley, will be there. You know he's opening a branch of the Fortune Foundation here."

Amelia smiled. "I know you're excited about that, but I suspect it's more because Christopher's moving back here from Red Rock."

"It was hard when he was gone," Jeanne Marie admitted. "When he left, there was such turmoil between him and Deke. All came to a head because of that darned money James Marshall wanted to give me." She let out a huge sigh as if she were dismissing all her bad thoughts and smiled again. "The important thing is our boy is coming home. Kinsley will be a beautiful wife for him and he's happier than he's ever been. He's finally found his niche with the Foundation."

"Tell me again how we're all connected to it?"

Jeanne Marie leaned against the porch rail, her expression bright. "Chris could tell you far more than I ever could since he works there, but it was founded in memory of Ryan Fortune who was a distant cousin of ours. They have all sorts of community programs and they help fund clinics and—oh, just bunches of good things for people. Having a branch in Horseback Hollow is going to mean so much. It'll be jobs, it'll be aid for those who need it—" Her eyes sparkled as she focused on Amelia's face. "Where was I? Oh, yes. Ryan's cousin William Fortune—he used to have a business in California—is married now to Lily, who was Ryan's widow and they're in Red Rock. I know it sounds scandalous, but it really wasn't. And then there are the Atlanta Fortunes—John Michael is our oldest brother, then James Marshall and your mama and me."

Amelia chuckled. "I need a map."

"I know." Jeanne Marie laughed merrily. "And they all have grown children and some of them are starting families, and it's just… Well, I hit the mother lode in family when I grew up with none except my adoptive parents."

Amelia smiled. It was hard not to let her aunt's delight infect her as well. "And to answer your question, yes, I'd love to join you all for dinner." She wasn't going to speak for Quinn.

Jeanne Marie glanced at her watch and tsked. "Speaking of, I've got to get the roasts in the oven or we'll be stuck eating at the Horseback Hollow Grill. Come by anytime. Food'll be on around six." She kissed Amelia's forehead and went back down the steps, briskly returning to her car.

Amelia watched her drive away, then jumped a little when Quinn appeared around the side of the house.

He was wearing a white T-shirt covered in sweat and dirt, multi-pocketed cargo shorts, heavy work boots and had a tool belt slung around his lean hips.

And he still needed a shave.

She felt heat gather inside her and dug her fingernails into her palms as a distraction.

It failed miserably, particularly when he spotted her hovering there on the front porch. It felt as if his gaze saw right through her dress to the sum total of nothing that she wore beneath it.

She pulled the strap that kept slipping off her shoulder back into place and snatched up the bag of clothes that Jeanne had delivered. "My aunt played personal shopper," she said.

The top rail surrounding the porch was chest high to him and he dropped his arm over it before tipping back the bill of the ball cap he wore. Throwing up in front of him may have been excruciatingly embarrassing, but it had served to break *some* of the tension.

At least he didn't have accusation clouding his eyes every time he looked at her.

"Guess you're wishing you'd have had her do that in the first place," he said

The bag crinkled in her fingers. "It would have been easier," she allowed. The memory of the way his T-shirt had torn the night before taunted her, and she focused instead on the dirt covering the one he was wearing now. "What, um, what have you been doing?"

He lifted his arm off the rail again and tilted his head. "Come on. I'll show you."

Surprised by the invitation, she squeezed the bag again. "I should, uh, probably change."

His lips quirked and he plucked his dirty shirt. "What for?"

She dragged her eyes away from his chest. "Aunt Jeanne invited us for dinner later."

"Nice of her. S'pose you want to go."

"Christopher will be there. I haven't seen him since Sawyer's wedding over New Year's. He's engaged now."

"I heard."

It wasn't an answer of whether *he* wanted to go. "So?"

He smiled faintly. "I generally don't turn down a meal cooked by someone else."

She didn't know if she was relieved or not. But she left the porch anyway.

He waited until she reached him before turning and heading away from the house and the barn and the antique-looking windmill beside it that stood motionless in the still summer air. They passed several pens, all empty and fenced in by round metal rails, following a path that was more dirt than gravel with a strip of grass growing down the center.

He kept to the dirt part and puffs of dust rose around his sturdy boots as he went and he eyed her when she moved to the grassier strip and shook one foot then the other to get out the grit that had worked its way into her sandals.

"These boots aren't made for walking," she said wryly.

"I could toss you over my shoulder," he deadpanned.

She flushed and continued walking. "I don't think so," she said primly.

He laughed softly.

Something in her stomach curled, and it was not morning sickness.

She stared ahead at the land. It seemed more covered in scrubby bushes and wild grasses than anything. And the horizon seemed to stretch forever. "Don't you have fences to pen in your cattle?"

"There's fence. Just can't see it from here."

"What about your horses?"

"We're getting there."

She moistened her lips. "It's, uh, it's very warm today, isn't it?"

He shot her an amused look. "Probably close to ninety. 'Bout average for this time of year. Be glad there's air-conditioning in the house. The one I grew up in didn't have it. Probably just as well that shack burned down. Made tearing down what was left easy."

"You told me back in April you were very young when it happened."

He shrugged. "Fifteen." The hammer hanging from his tool belt made a soft brushing sound against his khaki-colored cargos with each step he took and she realized her steps had slowed, intentionally or not, allowing her an excellent view of his backside.

She picked up her pace again, skipping a few times until she was level with him once more.

He didn't seem to notice.

"Same year my dad died," he added.

She studied his profile. The night of Toby's wedding, they'd talked about everything under the sun. But he hadn't told her that he'd been married. Or that the fire had happened the very same year he'd also lost his father. "That must have been devastating."

"You lost your dad, too."

"And it was horrible," she murmured, "but we still had a home."

"The Chesterfield estate," he drawled.

Her nerves prickled at his tone. "Yes."

He stopped. Propped his hands on his hips and stared out. "Lot different than this place, no doubt."

She continued forward a few steps and turned until she was facing him. "Yes," she agreed. "But, like the Rocking-U, it has been in the Chesterfield family for generations. I understand ancestral ties to one's land."

His lips twitched again.

"What?"

"Just listening to you talk, darlin'." He shook his head. "Kills me."

She huffed. "There is nothing wrong with the way I speak. *You* are the one who's all…all…drawly." Had he really called her *darlin'*?

"Drawly." His smile stretched. "That some grammatical term they taught you in those fancy schools you attended?" He shook his head again, then started walking once more, brushing past her since she was standing right in his path.

Wholly bemused, she turned and followed and shortly, the road began descending and she realized his house and his barn were positioned on the top of a ridge. "There's a river!"

"That's like calling a mosquito an eagle. It ain't a river, but it's a decent creek. The Rocking-U always had water and thank God it still does since Texas has been drying up around our ears for too damn long." He headed for the trees and the grass growing lush and thick alongside the glittering water.

She hurried after him. Several horses were grazing contentedly, barely even giving a flick of their tails at their approach. "It's beautiful down here."

He pointed at an enormous oak tree. "That is what I've been doing."

Confused, she walked toward the tree, feeling the coolness its shade provided. She had no idea how tall it was, but it was *huge,* with a trunk so wide not even Quinn could have circled it with his arms. "Pruning the tree?"

"Nah. Nature prunes that beast. Even lost a couple limbs during a lightning storm when I was a kid." He closed his hand around her upper arm and moved her around to one side, pointing up into the canopy above them. "You can still see the scar there."

She couldn't see anything because her entire being seemed focused on the feel of his fingers. "Right," she said faintly.

"Figured I'd build it back up."

"Hmm?"

He was still pointing and she mentally shook herself, looking. She saw the healed over slash on the trunk, nearly hidden among the leaves. And then she saw the pieces of lumber a few feet above that, forming the frame for a floor. "You're building a *tree house?*"

"Rebuilding." He let go of her, circling the base of the tree where she realized he'd fastened fresh boards for a ladder. "The one my dad put up was about like everything he put up." He looked wry. "Half-assed and half-done," he murmured. "But the guy never stopped trying."

Quinn's efforts were half-done, too, but that was the only comparison she could see. "I used to love climbing trees. I'd go as high as I could and feel like I was flying. My mother didn't agree. She used to send me to the nursery as punishment. Since I considered myself much too mature as a teen for that, it seemed a fate worse than death." She eagerly placed her foot on the first foothold.

"No way, princess. You're not climbing up there."

She huffed. "I'm perfectly capable!"

"You were perfectly capable of riding a bus all the way from Dallas, too, and look what state you were in once you got here."

He closed his hands around her hips and she went breathless, her nerves vibrating. But all he did was lift her away from the tree and set her feet on the thick grass. "You're pregnant," he added. "You're not going up there. The floor isn't close to being finished. What if you fell?"

Her lips parted. Why hadn't she realized that herself?

"But I want to go up there." She craned her head back and studied the tree house. It wasn't complete, of course, but when it was, she could tell it would be magnificent. "I think you have a bit of Peter Pan in you."

His expression sobered. "I grew up a long time ago."

"Why are you build—*re*building this now?"

He looked back up into the branches. "It was a good place to be when I was a kid."

She chewed the inside of her cheek, watching him. "And you think it'll be a good place for—"

"Our kid." His hazel gaze slid over her. "Yeah."

She was melting inside. There simply was no other description for it. "It'll be years before he—"

"Or she—"

"—is ready for that," she finished huskily.

"Yeah, well, it's also a good way to burn off some energy. And lately, I have a lot of—" He suddenly tugged the strap that had slipped from her shoulder back into place. "Energy."

Her mouth went dry and breathing became an effort. She stared up at him, feeling the warmth of him sliding around her, through her.

"What's this?" He dragged his finger along her collarbone where her skin was faintly irritated.

Her heart lurched. "I think it's, um—" She moistened her lips. "From your beard."

Something came and went in his eyes. He abruptly turned away and slapped his palm against the tree as he walked around it, heading toward the stream. "It'll be a good tree house," he said briskly.

She actually felt herself sway and was glad he was looking elsewhere. She hauled in a soundless breath and pressed her hand to her heart, willing it to calm. She'd blame the effect he had on her on pregnancy hormones if she could, but he'd had the same effect on her from the very beginning.

It's the reason she was pregnant in the first place.

"You coming?" He'd taken off his tool belt and sat down on the grass and was unlacing his boots. "Might as well cool off in the water for a few minutes."

She knew the water wasn't deep enough to swim; she could see right through the crystal clear water to the rocky bottom.

No skinny-dipping here.

She held back a nervous giggle at the shockingly disappointing thought and started toward him, only to trip a little when he tossed his cap aside and pulled his T-shirt over his head.

He glanced her way. "You all right?"

She balled her fists in the folds of the dress at her sides and smiled brightly. "Just shoe… Just caught my, uh, my shoe. In the grass."

He looked away but not before she saw his smile and she knew she was turning as red as the borrowed, too-oft-worn dress.

Pressing her lips together, she crossed the grass purposefully and sat down beside him. "Would serve you right if I whipped *my* dress over my head," she said crossly.

He laughed outright, tossing his T-shirt behind him. "Darlin', if you're expecting a protest from me, you're dreaming. Unless you took to stealing boxers from my drawer, I know what all you *don't* have on under there so feel free to get naked as a jaybird. No telephoto lens in the world strong enough to spot you out here."

Flushing even harder, she slid her feet out of the sandals and stuck them in the water. "Whoa!" She just as rapidly jerked them back. "Cold."

"Refreshing," he countered, and tugged off his boots and socks. Then he stood and stepped into the creek. The water swirled around his strong calves, only a few inches below the bottom of his long shorts. "Come on." He held out his hand and beckoned.

"What if I slip and *fall?*"

He smiled faintly. "I'm getting the sense you were pretty spoiled growing up. You're the baby of the lot, right?"

"Yes. And I was not spoiled," she grumbled and pushed to her feet, stepping gingerly into the water, bunching the dress in one hand above her knees.

After the initial shock, the water was possibly more refreshing than frigid, though she wasn't going to admit it. She was glad for his hand, though, because the rocks littering the bottom of the creek were smooth and slick.

"If you start to fall *here,*" he said calmly, "I would catch you." He squeezed her free hand.

And her heart squeezed right along with it.

They walked quite a distance and he kept to the center of the creek which she quickly discovered was far less rocky and far more sandy and she was able to let go of his hand and walk unaided.

When he finally stopped, he swept his arm from one side to the other. "All Rocking-U land right up to there." He pointed. "That water tower over there is the eastern border."

She could see the structure well off in the distance across an expanse of unyielding looking red earth peppered with stubby trees, wild grasses in every shade from olive to straw, and lazy-looking cattle in just as many hues from yellow to black with horns that looked deadly even from a distance. And the blue sky overhead went on and on, without a single cloud in sight.

In her mind's eye, she pictured him on horseback, riding out there. Open and free. "It's no wonder you came back," she breathed. "Built your house. Built your herd." She looked up to find him watching her.

"This life isn't for everyone."

She wasn't sure if he was warning her, or remembering. In April he'd told her how his mother had been happy to leave this place. "Maybe your mum couldn't bear staying after losing your dad."

"She wasn't the only one who didn't like it here." He touched her elbow but she didn't want to take the hint that it was time to turn back.

"You mean your ex-wife," she said instead. "She didn't go far," Amelia added boldly. "Jess told me she lives in Vicker's Corners."

His eyes were narrowed against the bright sun. "Might not seem like it to you, but there's a big difference between Horseback Hollow and Vicker's Corners."

Yes. Horseback Hollow possessed a single main street with a handful of businesses, though that was already changing with the coming Hollows Cantina and Fortune Foundation office. For now, Vicker's Corners, while still small and quaint, was considerably more developed.

"I like Horseback Hollow," she said evenly and sloshed her feet through the water, her toes squeezing into the sandy bottom as she started back the way they'd come.

For how long?

The question stuck in Quinn's head though he didn't

voice it. He watched her walking in front of him. She was holding up the dress, but the back of it had still dragged in the water below her knees, and it trailed behind her, dark and wet. Her hair was tangled around her shoulders that were turning pink from too much sun.

Right now, she might want to be there.

But she didn't know how hard his life could be. Didn't know that sometimes there could be as many bad years as good. That's what had driven his dad to his early grave.

Ahead of him, Amelia leaned down and swiped her hand through the water, then splashed it over her head.

She looked young. And carefree and ungodly sexy.

He blew out a harsh breath and leaned over, cupping water to throw over his own face. It was cold.

But it wasn't enough to douse the heat.

It wasn't ever going to be enough to do that.

Chapter Ten

"I was getting used to the red dress."

Amelia smiled ruefully as she entered the kitchen. Once they'd returned from their walk, Tanya was finished, so while Quinn paid the teenager, Amelia had gone upstairs to shower and change into the clothes that her aunt had procured for her while Quinn headed into the barn.

"This isn't going to fit me for long," she told him now and twitched the skirt that reached her ankles. The light gray knit hugging her hips before flaring out loosely had wide black stripes angled across it and was much livelier than her usual taste, but she'd toned it down with a white T-shirt with a deep scooped neck and snug cap sleeves. She knew the second she developed a bump, it would show. "The sundress was roomy enough to last awhile."

He was sprawled at the kitchen table wearing jeans

and a black T-shirt. He'd obviously used the downstairs bathroom to shower as well; his hair was wet and darker than ever. He'd also shaved.

She nearly told him she'd been getting used to the ridiculously sexy stubble.

"Not that it matters," she blathered on. "I'll have my own wardrobe soon enough."

He didn't move, but his gaze sharpened. "Is it being shipped here?"

She had the sense to realize she'd just stepped right into a minefield. All because she obviously couldn't think sensibly when she was near him.

"No," she said cautiously. "But I can't stay here forever."

"Here." His jaw canted slightly to one side for a moment. "Rocking-U here? Horseback Hollow here?" His eyes narrowed and he rose. It was like watching a cobra uncoil. "*United States* here?"

She stood her ground though the desire to back up was strong. "I do have responsibilities at home. I can't avoid them forever."

"I told you, I'm not letting you take my child away from here."

"Actually, to be specific," her tone cooled, "you said you weren't going to let another man raise your child."

He slowly pushed the chair back into the table. "What did I tell you about pulling that royal face with me?"

A jolt shot through her from her head to her toes.

She wisely took that step back after all, only to find her spine against the countertop. "I'm not pulling anything," she attempted reasonably. "I'm not saying I intend to return to the UK permanently."

"You want to go back, you can go. After we visit the justice of the peace."

"I don't have the choice of a minister anymore?" Her smart question fell flat and she exhaled. "At least you seem to believe me about James," she muttered.

He snorted. "Honey, I don't give a goddamn anymore if you were engaged to the man for real." He stepped up to her and pressed his palm flat against her abdomen. "The second you told me you're pregnant with *my* kid, that no longer mattered."

She braced herself against the shudder that rippled through her.

He angled his head toward hers. But all he did was speak softly next to her ear. "I may not be some fancy-pants future earl with money and connections, but there is no way on this earth I will let my child grow up without me." He suddenly straightened and dragged his palm upward until it was pressed flat between her breasts. Then he spread his fingers, rubbing them pointedly over the stab of her nipple through the white fabric. "I'll use every advantage I've got."

She couldn't very well deny the fact that she was weak where he was concerned. She'd slept with the man after only a few dances, something she'd never once been remotely tempted to do even though she'd been squired around by suitable matches since she was sixteen.

But neither could he hide the fact that he was equally aroused by her.

"Is that a threat?" she asked evenly. "Or a promise?"

His eyes darkened. "Don't pull an animal's tail, princess. Even the most patient one'll eventually turn on you."

The man who'd counted stars on a magical April

night with her was the same one who was building a tree house, and the same one who was standing here now, she reminded herself, and she lifted her chin.

"You already turned on me," she reminded boldly. "When I didn't immediately deny the engagement stories." Her heart was thundering so hard in her chest he couldn't fail to notice. "And whether that was wrong or not, you obviously didn't care about me as much as I'd believed, or you wouldn't have mistrusted me as easily as you did. And you *still* don't trust me, only this time it's because you think I'll take your child away from you."

Instead of trying to pull away, she leaned into him until her breasts were pressed against his chest, his hand caught between them. "I am not your ex-wife," she said evenly. "No matter what you thought, or still think for that matter, I didn't betray you with anyone. And I have no intention of keeping you from being this baby's father." She went onto her toes until her mouth was only inches from his. "Using sex," she whispered slowly, "still isn't going to make me agree to a loveless marriage."

Then, taking advantage of the fact that he'd gone still as a statue, she shimmied out from between him and the cabinet and deliberately lowered her gaze to the hard length of him clearly evident behind his zipper. "Now, are we going to my aunt's for dinner, or do you have something else in mind?"

His eyes narrowed until only a greenish-brown sliver showed. His jaw flexed. And for a breathless moment that seemed to last an eternity, she was afraid he would call her bluff.

But he finally moved and the sound of his boot against the tile floor seemed loud. "Be glad there's hardly any food in the fridge," he said, and pulled open the kitchen door, stomping outside.

Her shoulders sank and she brushed her hair behind her shoulders with shaking fingers.

"You waiting for a pumpkin carriage or something?" he called from outside.

She pressed her lips together, lifted her chin and joined him.

Deke and Jeanne Marie's place was so packed inside with people when Quinn and Amelia arrived that, at first, their entrance wasn't even noticed.

But then Piper, half crawling and half walking, latched on to Amelia's leg and she chuckled, picking up the little girl and stepping into the crowd of family, leaving Quinn behind.

He couldn't seem to drag his eyes away from her. The shirt she was wearing hugged her lithe torso like a lover, and the skirt was just as guilty around her narrow waist and slender hips. It hardly seemed possible that she was sheltering a baby inside her.

"You going to stand there and drool or do you want a beer?" Liam stood beside him looking amused.

Quinn took the beer bottle and twisted it open. He nodded toward Liam's younger brother, Christopher, who seemed to be holding court in the middle of the parlor, his arm around a pretty blonde. "Guess your family's going to be having a lot of weddings in the near future."

Julia, Liam's fiancée, tucked herself under Liam's arm. "We might have to draw dates out of a hat," she said humorously. But then she looked stricken, looking from Quinn's face to Amelia and back again.

He pretended not to notice.

All of Jeanne Marie and Deke's offspring were engaged except for Galen and Delaney. The oldest and the youngest. And Toby, as well. He and Angie had already gotten hitched.

He finally managed to pull his gaze away from the swell of Amelia's hips where she'd pulled the hem of her snug T-shirt over the long, flowing skirt. As a teenager, he'd always been more preoccupied with the front of a woman.

But the perfect sweep of Amelia's back, nipping into her waist then flaring out again was enough to bring him to his knees.

He chugged a little more beer. The front door was open, but the room was still too warm thanks to all the bodies. He asked the first thing he could think of. "Toby and Angie get their adoption approved yet?"

"Not yet." Almost absently, Liam brushed his lips against Julia's forehead as he looked over at his middle brother. He was sitting on the couch with Kylie on his knee, watching over the checker game that Brian and Justin were playing.

Quinn hadn't been around the Hemings kids all that much, but it was the quietest he'd ever seen them. "Never thought adoption proceedings took this long. Toby was already taking care of them for months before he filed."

"I don't think all adoptions have the challenges that Toby and Angie have had," Julia murmured.

"You'd think learning we're Fortune-connected would have made it easier," Liam added, even though Quinn could remember a time when his buddy hadn't been remotely thrilled about that particular connection. He'd been suspicious the Fortunes were invading Horseback Hollow, throwing their moneyed weight around and making too many changes. "Instead, the social worker's got some bug about the kids' safety *because* of it."

Christopher joined them, holding Kinsley's hand. "Yeah, well, there've been times over the years when being a Fortune was sort of like having a target painted on your chest. The stories I learned while I was in Red Rock—" He pursed his lips and blew. "Lot of history there. Some serious stuff."

"That was years ago," Liam dismissed.

"Tell that to Gabriella," Julia reminded. "She only came to Horseback Hollow to take care of her dad after his plane accident. And those anonymous letters to the post office, saying it wasn't an accident? That it was sabotage and the *Fortunes* were the target and not Mr. Mendoza at all?" She made a face. "You'd think people around here would be grateful your cousin Sawyer and his wife opened their flight school and charter service in Horseback Hollow instead of somewhere else. I'm sure the investigators will get to the bottom of things, but what a horrible business."

"You gonna let that scare you off of marrying me? My mama's a Fortune, too," Liam goaded lightly, clearly not afraid of any such thing.

Julia's eyebrows rose. "Oh, no," she assured. "You're not getting off the matrimonial hook, mister, any more than Jude is with Gabi."

Quinn sucked down half the beer. Everyone around him seemed as happy as pigs wallowing in mud. He wished he found it revolting.

Instead he just found it…enviable.

His gaze strayed back to Amelia. She was perched on the arm of her aunt's chair, still holding Piper on her lap and trying to untangle the kid's fingers from her long hair.

She couldn't be accustomed to gatherings like this. Nearly twenty people jammed into the front parlor of an old ranch house. The night they'd spent together she'd told him about the huge house where she'd grown up. The servants. The carefully orchestrated public functions.

What reason would be strong enough to keep her in Texas when she had *ancestral lands* and a family estate and God knew what else waiting for her back home?

It wasn't love.

She'd already said as much. No loveless marriages for her.

One small sliver of his mind kept listening to the conversation around him.

"Has Toby been able to find out who made that donation to him yet?" someone asked.

"Don't think he cares. That anonymous money'll go a long way to raising those kids. There's enough for college funds even."

"Must be nice," Quinn murmured. Generally speaking, there weren't too many packed into that parlor who'd been able to go to college at all. Or, like him, they'd had to scrimp and save and pray for every scholarship that came their way.

Not Amelia, though.

She'd gone to the finest schools that her family's money and position could buy.

Through no effort of his, her baby—his baby—would never want for anything.

He'd finished his beer and needing escape he excused himself, heading into the kitchen that was nearly as congested as the parlor. Jeanne Marie was at the center of things, giving out orders to her helpers with the precision of a master sergeant. She caught his eye with a smile as he continued right on through until he'd escaped out the back where Deke and Galen were hanging over the opened hood of an old pickup truck.

He joined them. "You still trying to keep this old thing running, eh?"

"Never get rid of something that still works." Deke's hands were covered in grease as he worked.

"*Works* being the operative word here," Galen said wryly. His hands weren't quite as filthy as his dad's but they were close. Quinn still shook the man's hand when he stuck it out, then propped his elbows on the side of the truck to watch them tinker.

"Guess that reporter girl has been making the rounds in town," Galen said. "Has she found her way out to the Rocking-U yet?"

Quinn grimaced. "Don't expect her to. She only knew to find Amelia here because it's no secret Jeanne's her aunt." He absently grabbed a hose that Deke couldn't quite reach and held it in place.

"What's going on between you two?" Deke pinned Quinn with a look. "Jeanne Marie's real fond of that gal. Do I need to ask your intentions?"

Galen laughed silently and lifted his hands up. "Good luck, bro. I'm outta here." He turned on his heel and strode away.

Deke's brows rose. "Well?"

"You don't need to ask," he said flatly.

"Recognize the side of my own house when I see it," the other man said.

He damned the heat rising in his neck. "Jeanne know about the photo, too?"

The other man's eyebrow rose. "Who d'ya think showed it to me?"

Quinn grimaced. "She's not engaged to that other guy."

"Heard that, too. Amelia 'fessed up on that score to Jeanne Marie right off," he added at Quinn's surprised look.

"She comes from a different world," Quinn said after a moment.

"Yup," Deke agreed, drawing out the word. He scratched his cheek, leaving behind a streak of black. "You worried about that?"

Quinn started to deny it but the older man's steady gaze wouldn't let him. "Yes, sir."

"Yeah." Deke's piercing gaze finally flicked past Quinn to look at the house behind them. "Jeanne Marie coulda bought anything her heart desired if she'd kept that money her brother wanted to give her. Clothes. New car. New furniture. Coulda travelled around the world a dozen times and stayed in the fanciest hotels there are. Hard to figure why a woman wouldn't care about those things but she says she doesn't." He pursed his lips for a second and scratched his cheek again.

"Deke Jones!"

They both looked back to see Jeanne Marie hanging out the screen door. "You get your hands outta that rust bucket and wash up for supper!"

Deke straightened and wiped his hands on a thin red rag he pulled from the back pocket of his jeans. He smiled a little at Quinn and tossed the rag to him. "All comes down to trust," he said and headed toward the house.

It was easy for Deke to trust Jeanne, Quinn thought,

wiping his hands and following. They'd been married longer than he'd been alive.

The first time he'd set eyes on Amelia had been six months ago. And he could count on his fingers how many actual days they'd spent together in the time since.

He pulled open the screen door and went inside. Jeanne Marie was smiling up into Deke's face, rubbing a dish towel over the black streak on the man's weathered cheek. "What am I going to do with you?" he heard her murmuring.

"Don't you want to be like them after forty years together?"

Startled, Quinn found Stacey and Colton standing behind him and he realized her words had been for her fiancé. He gave them a dry look.

"Considering the two of you can't look at each other without a besotted expression on your face, I'd say your chances are pretty good," Quinn said.

Colton chuckled and Stacey smirked, jerking her chin toward the doorway opening up to the dining room where Amelia was standing, talking to her cousin Jude and Gabriella. "Get out a mirror whenever you're looking *her* way," Stacey suggested smartly.

"Dishes, dishes," Jeanne Marie called out. "If you are standing in *this* kitchen, and your hands are empty, then grab something and take it into the dining room," she ordered. "Meal's not going to get onto the table by itself!"

Quinn grabbed the closest thing—a basket of fragrant, yeasty rolls—and escaped into the dining room.

They'd had to set up folding card tables on either end of the actual dining room table to accommodate everyone but they were covered with tablecloths. None of them matched. Some had colorful flowers stitched on the corners. Some didn't. But they were all crisply ironed and Quinn had a sudden memory of the way his mom had stood at an ironing board doing just the same thing before every Thanksgiving and every Christmas. The plates weren't all matching, either, nor were the glasses, but they were Jeanne's best.

She had all of her family home and it was obvious that she was celebrating that fact with all the finery she had.

She bustled in to the crowded room, pointing and directing and soon everyone's butt was in their designated chair. Deke at the head of the pushed-together tables. Jeanne Marie at the opposite.

Quinn and Amelia were situated midway down, next to each other. The chairs—another mixture of real dining room chairs, folding chairs and even the picnic table bench from outdoors—made for cozy seating, and there was barely two inches to spare between them and that, only because Amelia was as narrow and slender as she was.

Deke said the blessing and the dishes started passing. Quinn was relieved to see Amelia pile on the food for once. She was too thin as it was, and now she was eating for two. And fortunately, there were so many simultaneous conversations going on that nobody seemed to notice the fact that they were barely participating.

Her arm brushed his when they both reached for the cucumber salad at the same time and she quickly drew back. "Excuse me."

He grabbed the bowl and held it for her. "Go ahead."

Her gaze flicked over his, then away again. She scooped some of the salad onto her plate. "I feel like a glutton," she murmured as she handed him the handle of the serving spoon.

"It's about time you're finally eating more than a few bites." He dumped some of the cucumber and onion mixture on his plate. His mom made the same thing every time he visited her in Dallas. "Were you the one who gave that money to Toby for the kids?" He kept his voice low so only she would hear.

She blinked, looking genuinely surprised. "No." She looked across and down the tables. Toby's brood was surrounding one of the folding tables, with him and Angie on either side.

Supervising referees, he figured.

"Even if I'd wanted, *I* don't personally have that kind of money," she said quietly. "From what Aunt Jeanne told me, it was quite a large sum. It wasn't my mum, either. Aunt Jeanne asked her outright."

"How much money do you have?"

She let out a soft sound and gave him another quick look. "Why are you asking?"

He just eyed her. "Why do you think?"

Her soft lips compressed. "This is hardly the time, Quinn."

"Preacher or justice of the peace?" He waited a beat. "If you can't make up your mind, we could put it out for a vote right here. See what everyone else has to say."

Beneath the edge of the starchy white tablecloth, she dug her fingertips into his thigh. "You wouldn't dare."

He damned the heat collecting in his gut and closed his hand over her wrist, pushing her hand away. "Don't tempt me." The warning worked on all counts. Outing her pregnancy to the entire family all at once. Pulling her hand up to his fly despite sitting in the middle of that very family.

She twisted her wrist free. "I have a personal account

that I control," she said after a moment. "It allows me a comfortable existence."

"Comfortable's a subjective term."

"Comfortable," she repeated evenly. "Not extravagant. Then there are family trusts as well from both my mother's and my father's sides that my brothers and sister and I all come into at various ages. It's all managed and very secure, and frankly I haven't ever much thought about it." She speared a green bean with her fork and smiled tightly. "Does that answer your question?"

Enough to underline the differences between their worlds.

Even if he sold every acre of Rocking-U land, and every hoof that ran on it, he wouldn't be able to match the resources she had at her disposal.

Amelia suddenly grabbed his hand beneath the table and pressed it against her belly. "I am not taking him away," she murmured, sliding him a look. "Now, quit looking shocked and eat your supper."

Chapter Eleven

By the time they returned to the Rocking-U it was late.

Quinn parked where he usually did halfway between the house and the barn and turned off the engine. "Your aunt's a good cook," he said after a moment and felt the look Amelia gave him.

"Maybe she'll give me lessons," she said. "It'd be more useful than most of the other lessons I've had." She pushed open the door herself and got out, heading around the truck toward the house.

His neck prickled, though he didn't really know why and his eyes searched out the shadows of the barn and the windmill.

But there was nothing to see.

That's what came from studying every unfamiliar car he spotted. Every unfamiliar face. He was letting paranoia get the best of him.

He left the keys hanging in the ignition like always and caught up to her. "Let me turn on a light first." He went up the front steps and inside. Turned on the porch light and held the door open for her. His gaze roved over the porch. The two rocking chairs his mom had given him a few Christmases ago were in their usual spot. Nothing out of place.

Amelia slipped past him. "What's wrong?"

He rubbed the back of his neck and closed the door. "Nothing." He hit the wall switch again, turning on the light that hung over the small foyer.

"You should take the bed tonight." She folded her arms around herself. "It's your bed. And the sofa is too short for you."

The simple answer squatted like a fat elephant in the middle of the room.

Share the bed.

"I'll live." Once she was gone—and he was convinced she would be sooner or later—he'd need to get rid of the couch, too. Like the bed, it would be riddled with memories. "I'm gonna take a look around outside."

Amelia studied him for a moment. He was still rubbing the back of his neck. "Seriously, Quinn. What's wrong?"

"Nothing," he said again and went into the kitchen to retrieve the shotgun from the rack over the door. "Just want to check if that possum's rooting around again." He went outside before she could comment.

Sighing, Amelia wrapped her hand around the banister and dragged herself upstairs.

She'd never felt so tired in her life and wanted to blame it entirely on being pregnant. But feeling like she was on one side of a war with Quinn on the other was not helping.

She washed her face and cleaned her teeth—blessing her aunt who'd had the forethought to include some basic toiletries among the clothes—and pulled on the pinstriped shirt of Quinn's again for something to sleep in. She bundled up the quilt—it was warm enough that a person didn't need any covering but a sheet anyway—and carried it downstairs, along with one of the bed pillows.

She didn't care what Quinn said. He was over six feet tall and couldn't possibly stretch out comfortably on the sofa. He needed his own sleep, too.

She spread the quilt out on the brown cushions, then flopped down on it, bunching the pillow under the back of her neck. She yawned hugely and pressed her hands to her belly.

How long would it be before it was no longer flat?

Before her secret—*their* secret—was visible for anyone and everyone to see?

How long would it be before Quinn would trust her?

She flexed her toes against the arm at the end of the sofa, and yawned again before turning on her side, cradling the pillow to her cheek, and slept.

She didn't even wake when Quinn came in a while later and spotted her sleeping on the couch.

He hadn't found the possum, though the evidence it had been there was obvious thanks to the trash can it had upended and strewn across the ground in back of the barn.

He'd cleaned up the mess, slammed the lid back on the can and weighted it down again with a concrete block. He should've remembered to warn Tanya to do the same when she was cleaning.

Now, looking at Amelia's defiant possession of the couch, he debated the wisdom of carrying her upstairs and putting her in bed where she belonged.

Some remaining cells of common sense inside his brain laughed at that. There *was* no wisdom in carrying Amelia anywhere. He'd already proven that.

Sleeping in his own bed without her—now that she'd occupied it twice—held zero appeal but it was safer than the alternative.

He returned the shotgun to its rack, turned on the light over the stove so it wouldn't be completely dark if she woke, then turned off the foyer light and went upstairs.

Evidence of her was everywhere.

In the damp hand towel she'd folded neatly over the rack next to the sink

In the inexpensive clothes she'd folded and stacked on the top of his dresser in the bedroom.

For someone who'd grown up with servants at her beck and call, she was a whole lot neater than he was.

He flipped off the light and peeled out of his clothes, pitching them in the general direction of the hamper. It was stupid to be avoiding his own bed, but there was no denying that's what he was doing when he went to the window and fiddled with the blinds. Pulling them up. Letting them down. Tilting them until they were just so and then repeating the whole damn process again.

Finally, he gave up. He pulled on a pair of ancient sweatpants and went back downstairs and scooped Amelia off the couch.

She mumbled unintelligibly, turned her nose into his neck as trusting as a babe and slept on.

He carefully carried her upstairs and settled her on the center of his bed. It let out its faint, familiar squeak.

He started to back away, but she made a protesting sound and caught his arm.

Not asleep after all.

"I wish we could start over," she whispered.

So did he.

But he was afraid he wouldn't know how to do anything differently the second time around.

She pulled slightly on his arm. "Quinn."

He exhaled roughly and nudged her. "Move over."

She quickly wriggled over a few inches.

He lowered himself onto the mattress. "Come here." His voice was gruff.

She scooted back, until she was tucked against his side, her arm sneaking across his chest.

He stared into the dark. "We're getting a marriage license tomorrow." He wasn't sure if he said it to piss her off or to remind himself how adamantly opposed to marrying him she was.

She shifted slightly, but surprised him by not moving away. "Did your parents love each other?"

"What?"

"I always knew my parents loved each other," she whispered. "It was obvious in everything they did. He'd walk in a room and she'd light up. She'd smile at him when he was upset about something and place her hand on his chest, and everything would be all right." Her palm slid over his skin, leaving a trail of heat in its wake.

He steeled himself against it. "Get to the point, Amelia."

"That's what I want," she finished huskily. "The whole package. Can you give me that?"

His jaw was tight. "My father was illegitimate. I know that stuff doesn't matter these days, not like it used to.

But it mattered to his mother. It mattered to my old man. And it matters to me. You're having my kid. He's going to come into this world with my name. Nobody's going to steal that right from me. Not even you."

Pressing her hand against his chest, she levered herself up until she was half sitting. He could feel the weight of her gaze just as clearly as he could feel the long ends of her silky hair drifting over his ribs. "I'm not trying to steal anything, Quinn."

"Then prove it. Minister or justice of the peace?"

Her fingertips flexed against him with frustration, but only succeeded in sending heat through his veins.

"That's all marriage is to you? A means of legitimizing our baby? It has nothing to do with love?"

"Love's never been a friend of mine."

She was silent for so long he hoped she'd drop it.

But she didn't.

"If I said yes, what happens after the baby is born? What then? We live our separate lives? Passing the baby back and forth on what? Alternate weekends and holidays?"

His jaw went so tight it ached. "If that's the way you want it," he said stiffly. "You're used to a life that I won't ever be able to give you. Things I'll never be able to provide."

She was silent again for a long, long while before speaking, and when she did, her voice was husky. Careful. "I told you before that none of those…trappings… mattered to me. Did you…never believe me?"

"It's one thing to talk about it. It's another to actually live it."

Her fingers curled against him, then pulled away. "Be

glad I'm too exhausted to fight." She lay back down on the bed, her back to him.

Fighting was safer than making love.

He threw his arm over his eyes, grimly aware that there was no point in doing either.

And equally aware that it would only take a nudge, and he'd be ready for both.

He didn't expect to sleep, but eventually he did and when he woke it was only because his arm was going to sleep where it was tucked beneath Amelia's cheek and the rest of him was wide-awake thanks to her warm thigh tucked between his.

For a while, he stared at the sunlight streaking through the slats in the window blind. It had been years since he'd slept past dawn.

Then he carefully extricated himself, arms and legs, grabbed a pair of jeans and a shirt and left the room, quietly pulling the door closed after him.

He showered, letting the cold water pour over him, then pulled on his jeans and went downstairs. His mind consumed with the woman upstairs, he went through his usual routine by rote. Started water running through the coffeemaker. Dumped cereal into a bowl and ate it, standing in the back doorway, looking out over his land while it brewed. He had stock to check, horses to feed. Same things as every other day. Day in. Day out.

It was a life he loved. A life he knew he couldn't exchange for anything else, not unless he wanted his soul to shrivel up and die.

He heard a faint noise and looked back to see Amelia shuffling into the room, her eyes soft with sleep, her hair tangled and the shirt Jess had given him for his last birthday wrinkling around her bare thighs.

"Coffee smells so lovely." Her bare feet crossed the kitchen floor and she leaned over the coffeemaker, inhaling deeply.

The shirttails had climbed a few inches as she'd leaned against the counter and he dragged his eyes away from the smooth thighs and the tender spot behind her knees that he knew from experience was ticklish.

He knew his sister didn't drink any caffeine when she was pregnant. She also always gave up the margaritas she loved, and she'd complained often and long about that fact. Particularly since her husband, Mac, hadn't had to give up either.

"Sorry." He crossed the room and yanked the plug out of the outlet. The gurgling continued for only a moment before sputtering to a stop. "I'll quit making it."

She pushed her hair out of her face. Her gaze roved over his face. "You don't have to do that."

"Because you don't plan to be around?"

She tucked her hands behind her, leaning back against the counter. Unplugged and half-brewed or not, the scent of coffee filled the room. Same as her beauty shined through whether she was clothed in designer dresses or a man's wrinkled shirt.

"Because there's no reason for you to give up something you enjoy just because of me." She tucked her hair behind her ear. She wore no earrings. Didn't even have pierced ears at all. He knew, because he'd spent enough time kissing his way around her perfect earlobes to know there were no holes marring them. "There's no—" She broke off when there was a loud knocking on the front door.

He didn't want to answer it. Didn't much care who was out there, because he wasn't expecting anyone.

But she'd pressed her soft lips together and her lashes had swept down and whatever she'd been about to say was obviously going to go unsaid.

Particularly when the knocking continued, intrusively annoying and noisy as hell.

He left the kitchen and strode to the front door. "Cool your jets," he said, yanking it open.

He barely realized there were at least a half dozen people crammed onto his porch because of the cameras suddenly flashing and the microphone that was shoved close to his face.

"Do you have anything to say about your involvement with Amelia Chesterfield when her fiancé is reportedly sitting by his father's deathbed?"

Amelia suddenly raced up behind him and slammed the door shut on the words that just continued shouting through the wood.

Her eyes were huge in her face and she was visibly shaking. "How do they keep *finding* me?"

"I don't—" He broke off, because they were pounding on his door again and one of 'em—a guy with spiky hair and wide-lensed camera—was even peering through the unadorned front window.

Quinn grabbed Amelia's arm and steered her toward the staircase which was out of view from the window. "Stay."

"Don't aggravate them," she insisted, though she backed up several steps before sinking down onto one and hugging her arms around her knees. "It only makes them behave more outrageously." Her teeth were chattering and she'd gone white. "Did you tell anyone I was pregnant? Your sister? *Any*one? If that gets out—"

"I haven't told anyone," he said flatly.

The pounding and questions hadn't ceased and he stomped into the kitchen. He grabbed his shotgun off the rack above the doorway and loaded it with birdshot.

"What are you doing?"

She bolted to her feet and her huge eyes engulfed her entire face. They were the haunted eyes she'd had when she'd fainted in his barn.

And they made him want to string somebody up from the nearest tree.

"Getting rid of the vermin."

She shook her head rapidly. "Don't, Quinn. You have to ignore—"

"They're trespassing. Maybe they should've concerned themselves with aggravating *me*," he finished harshly.

Then he yanked open the door, greeting the intruders with the business end of the shotgun. "Get off my land."

Like cockroaches hit with the light, they scrambled off his porch, but only so far as to shield themselves.

He stepped out onto the wood porch and cocked the gun. It sounded satisfyingly loud and threatening. "Get."

"How long have you been sleeping with her?" some fool called out and Quinn swung the barrel toward the voice, finding the gel-haired guy who'd had the nerve to aim a camera through his front window.

"You're trespassing," he said coldly. "And I'm a real good shot." He met the man's eyes. At least he had the good sense to take a nervous step backward. "You want to test it out?"

"Lord Banning's a powerful man," someone else

yelled in a shrill voice. "You're not afraid of retribution for trying to steal his bride?"

He aimed beyond them where the vehicles they'd arrived in were parked every which way all over his gravel, and planted a load of shot exactly six inches from the front tire of the closest car. The noise was shockingly loud and gravel spewed, pinging against the car.

The roaches scattered even faster.

"Next one goes in the car!"

He had no intention of shooting anyone, but they didn't need to know that. There were seven of them, three men and four women, and he wondered which one, if any, was the Ophelia who'd plagued Amelia.

He eyed them each before cocking the gun again. *"Get off my land."*

They scrambled for the cars, nearly colliding among themselves as they poured into doors, gunned engines and spun tires.

Only when the last of them was nearly out of sight and the clouds of dust were starting to die did his grip on the gun relax.

And it was several minutes after that before the rest of him relaxed enough that he could go back inside the house.

He closed and locked the door, unloaded the rest of the birdshot and left the gun propped against the door.

Amelia was no longer huddled and hiding on the staircase.

She was pacing around the living room, looking agitated. "You couldn't have just *ignored* them? You had to go all…all Texas Ranger on them?" She sank down on the couch and clawed her fingers through her hair. "You may know ranching, Quinn, but I know the paparazzi.

There will be pictures of you on every network by the evening news." Just as fast as she'd sat, she shoved off the couch. "I have to phone my mother. Warn her." She laughed, sounding on the verge of hysteria, and her face was white. "If she hasn't already been treated to the same sorts of questions."

He caught her arms before she made it to the kitchen. "Calm down," he said. "You're going to make yourself sick again."

"Calm down?" She shook off his hands. "Would you feel calm if you knew you were causing nothing but embarrassment to the people you love?"

The words felt like blows.

"That's what involvement with me is. An embarrassment."

She looked stricken. "No! I never said that. I—I—" She broke off hugging her arms tightly around her. Her eyes turned wet. "I don't like being the cause of scandal. That's all."

"I don't believe you."

Her lips parted. She seemed to sway a little.

Then her face smoothed, though her eyes still gleamed, wet and glassy. "Of course you wouldn't," she said expressionlessly. "You haven't believed me about anything I've said yet. You just want to maneuver me into marriage to protect *your* interests. Same thing James wanted to do."

"You're gonna compare our baby to a textile company?"

She just shook her head, looking weary, and walked over to the stairs.

There was no phone upstairs. The only one inside the house hung on the wall in the kitchen.

"Thought you were calling your mother."

She didn't answer him. Just kept going up the stairs.

He was still standing there, rooted in place, when she came down a few minutes later.

She'd twisted her hair into a knot at the nape of her neck and pulled on a black T-shirt with the same striped skirt she'd worn the day before. The clothes were inexpensive. Hardly fancy. Yet she still managed to look untouchably elegant.

Her eyes didn't meet his. "If you'd be kind enough to drive me to Aunt Jeanne's, I would be grateful."

His hands curled into fists. "Aren't you afraid the vultures will be waiting?"

"I'm sure they will be." Her triangular chin lifted. "I'll handle it."

Unlike him.

She didn't say it.

But she didn't need to.

Chapter Twelve

"When is this going to die down?" Jeanne Marie fretted, and turned off the television and yet another gossipy tidbit on the morning news speculating about the most intimate details of Amelia's, Quinn's and James's lives while a silent video ran in the background showing Amelia, dressed only in Quinn's shirt slamming his front door shut on the photographers' cameras. "It's been a week already."

This time, the commentator—Amelia refused to call the vapid woman an actual reporter—had even dug up ancient stories about her mother's first marriage to Rhys Henry Hayes and even more ancient stories about King Edward's abdication of the throne for the woman he'd loved. Trying to manufacture out of thin air similarities where there were none at all.

"It's because of the funeral," Amelia said on a sigh.

James's father's funeral service had been held in London that morning and the timing made it a prime topic for the morning's national news shows. "The story will lose traction eventually, once something more interesting in the world comes along." She made a face. "Horrible of me to wish for a slew of natural disasters somewhere in the world."

Jeanne Marie squeezed her hand and sat down beside her. "Have you spoken with Quinn?"

Just the sound of his name caused a pang inside her and she shook her head.

Since he'd dropped her off at her aunt's home that dreadful morning a week ago, he hadn't tried to reach her once.

To be fair, she hadn't tried to speak with him, either. The only thing she'd been able to do was unleash threats of a lawsuit against the offenders who'd trespassed on the Rocking-U.

Only because her family had won the last suit they'd brought against the phone hackers a year ago had there been enough teeth behind the threat to encourage many of the pests to finally move on. Amelia wished that were true of Ophelia Malone, but the woman was still taking up residence at the B and B in Vicker's Corners. She was a freelancer, according to the sketchy information Molly had been able to unearth. She didn't have publishers keeping her on a leash they could retract when necessary.

"You're going to want to talk to Quinn sooner or later," her aunt said gently.

"I know." Amelia plucked the knee of her jeans. She just didn't know what she was going to say when she did. He'd had an up close and personal taste of the sort of things she'd had to deal with almost daily back in London.

Who would blame him for wanting no part of it?

For the past week, she'd lived in the seclusion of her aunt and uncle's house. Avoiding going outdoors in case there were still remaining telephoto lenses aimed their way. Avoiding all but the most necessary of phone calls. She'd even been careful not to find herself standing or sitting near windows.

It wasn't fair to burden her aunt and uncle with that sort of behavior, but they'd both been adamant that she remain with them. Even Amelia's mother had agreed that Amelia should stay in the States while she and James—now the Earl of Estingwood himself—dealt with the official media back home.

Everyone around her was taking care of her.

And she was heartily tired of it.

"I need a good solicitor," she said abruptly. "An attorney. Is there anyone you recommend? Someone you trust?"

Jeanne Marie looked thoughtful. "We haven't had a lot of need for attorneys, but Christopher once mentioned an attorney in Red Rock he knew through people at the Fortune Foundation. Or I can contact James Marshall. He surely has his own legal department at his company."

Amelia knew that JMF Financial was located in Georgia. Red Rock, though, was only four hundred or so miles away. "Would you mind calling Christopher for me?"

"Of course not." Jeanne Marie hesitated a moment. "Do you want me to call him right away?"

Now that Amelia had brought it up, she did.

In fact, she was suddenly impatient to do *something*.

"If you would. I need an appointment as soon as possible. Preferably before Mum arrives in a few days. I can call Sawyer Fortune and arrange for a charter flight to Red Rock." Until her latest escape from London and subsequent trek making her way to Quinn's, she'd used the flight service her cousin ran to get from Dallas to Horseback Hollow the other times she'd visited.

"You're ready to go out in public?"

Amelia made a face. "No," she admitted. "But the longer I hide out, the harder it will get. And I'd rather get used to it now than wait until the Cantina's grand opening this Friday." She followed her aunt into the kitchen and found herself looking out one of the windows at the picnic table and benches sitting on the grass.

But she wasn't really seeing them.

She was remembering dancing with Quinn out there on a portable dance floor.

He'd put his arms around her, and even though it was the first time he'd touched her, the first time they'd ever done anything but see each other from a distance really, she felt like she'd come home.

Her throat tightened and her nose burned with unshed tears.

Now, she feared that home was nothing more than a fantasy. A silly girl's romantic longing.

"Pour another." Quinn tapped the empty shot glass sitting on the bar in front of him. At seven in the evening, he hadn't expected the Two Moon Saloon to be entirely empty, even on a Tuesday. But he'd been the only one there for a good hour now.

He'd had no particular desire to go out at all, but Jess had nagged him into meeting up at the Horseback Hollow Grill for burgers with her family. He'd been avoiding her, like he'd been avoiding most everyone else in town for the past week. But he'd been sick of his own company, and since the paparazzi that had plagued him for most of the week since the whole shotgun incident had finally gone off for greener pastures, he'd agreed.

And even though, for once, his sister had wisely showed the good sense not to bring up anything to do with Amelia or the fact that his image—shirtless and brandishing a shotgun like some kind of madman—was all over creation thanks to the magic of the worldwide web and nonstop news services, he'd been glad when the meal was over.

While his sister and brother-in-law had corralled their sons out the door to go home, he'd just gone next door to the saloon that was attached to the grill.

He was sick of his own company, true. But he also wasn't in the mood for socializing.

Nor was he in the mood to hide out inside his own damn house because everywhere he looked, he saw Amelia.

One night last week he'd even slept out on the porch.

Damned pathetic.

He eyed the pretty bartender who was pouring him another shot of bourbon. "You're new." She had brown hair and brown eyes, just as dark as Amelia's, and was slender as a reed, also like Amelia.

And he didn't feel the faintest jangle of interest.

"What's your name?"

"Annette."

"Why'd you come to Horseback Hollow, Annette?" He tossed back the drink and clenched his teeth against the burn that worked down his throat. "Nothing going on in this place." He set the shot glass down on the wood bar with a thud.

She swiped her white bar towel over the wood. "Wouldn't say that, Mr. Drummond," she countered.

He narrowed his eyes, studying her while his fingers turned the small glass in circles on the bar. "How'd you know my name?"

She smiled faintly. "How d'ya think? I have a television." She lifted the bottle. "Another?"

He moved his hand away and she filled the glass, then set the bottle on the counter behind her and returned to her polishing.

"It wasn't as bad as it looked," he muttered.

"It looked like a man trying to protect what's his," she said calmly. "What's so bad about that?"

He lifted the glass, studying the amber-colored contents. The deputy sheriff who'd come calling about the matter had agreed with that notion and it'd been plain from the ample video coverage that Quinn hadn't tried shooting at anyone.

But that didn't change things for Quinn.

Amelia *wasn't* his. She'd made it plain she didn't want to be his. The only thing that *was* his was the baby she carried.

His chest tightened and hating the feeling, he put the glass to his lips. The liquor burned again, but brought no relief. No blurring of reality. No softening of the facts.

Amelia came from one world. He came from another.

"Send us over a round of margaritas and a couple a' waters, would you, darlin'?"

He realized that a group of people were coming in through the street-side entrance and glanced over to see Sawyer and Laurel Fortune coming in along with a few of the folks he knew were working for them over at their charter service. He lifted his hand, returning the greeting they sent him, then turned back to his solitude.

He quickly realized, though, that Sawyer and his group weren't cooperating with that notion, insisting that he join them as well.

Quinn had no desire to be among the Fortunes, but Orlando Mendoza was with them, and his daughter Gabriella was marrying Jude Fortune Jones, whom he'd known all his life. The new bartender was noisily scooping ice into margarita glasses with one hand and pouring tequila into a pitcher with the other so he reluctantly left his empty shot glass and moved over to their table.

"Y'all look like you're celebrating," he greeted.

"We are." Sawyer gestured to his companions. "You know everyone here, don't you, Quinn?"

"Some, more 'n others." Quinn gave a general nod, sticking out his hand to Orlando and the older man shook it. "Glad to see you're up on your feet again."

The pilot grinned. "Needed to if I'm going to be able to walk Gabi down the aisle and give her away when she and Jude get married. Glad to get the casts off at last. Things were itching me like crazy."

The bartender delivered the tray of waters and ice-filled, salt-rimmed glasses and set the margarita pitcher in the middle of the table before returning behind the bar.

"Broke my arm once." Quinn shook his head when Laurel started pouring out drinks and offered him one. "Couldn't stand the cast so bad I ended up cutting it off myself a week before the doctor said. Are you cleared for flying again?"

The salt-and-pepper-haired man nodded, looking relieved.

"That's what we're celebrating," Sawyer said. "That and the fact that the investigators have finally closed the case about the accident." He held up one of the glasses and waited while the others did the same. "No sabotage. No pilot error—" he gave a nod toward Orlando at that "—and no maintenance insufficiencies."

"So what happened?"

"Aircraft design," Orlando supplied.

"The plane's been recalled," Laurel added. She clinked her glass against her husband's and the others. "Just wish the manufacturer could have caught their error before people got hurt."

"Manufacturer is wishing the same thing," Sawyer said. "Not saying we're planning to, but it's a given that someone will bring lawsuits against them about it all."

Laurel looked at Quinn. "Speaking of lawsuits, is that what Amelia's planning?"

His skin prickled. "What do you mean?"

Orlando sat forward. He was the only one around the table drinking only water. "I flew Miss Chesterfield to Red Rock this morning. She was meeting with one of my cousin Luis's boys. Rafe's a lawyer over there. Told her she could've just waited until this weekend to talk to him, since he'll be in town for the opening of his brother's restaurant, but she was anxious to go now. I'll be picking her up again tomorrow afternoon."

Was she just adding on another layer of protection against more media invasions like they suspected? Or was she really laying the groundwork to keep his child away from him? "You'd have to ask Amelia what she's planning," he said abruptly and started backing away from the table. "I'll leave y'all to your celebrating. Congratulations." Not leaving them an opportunity to respond, he peeled a few bills off his wallet and dropped them on the bar.

Annette tucked the bills in the cash register. "You want some coffee before you head out, Mr. Drummond?"

He had never felt more stone-cold sober but to keep her satisfied and quiet about it, he told her to give him one to go, and then he went on his way, a foam cup of hot coffee in his hand. He was parked on the other side of the grill, so instead of leaving on the street side, he walked through the doorway separating the bar from the grill.

Only a few people were still sitting at the old-fashioned tables positioned around the ancient tiled floor. The little game room where his nephews always fought over playing the race car game was silent, the light turned off.

The coffee smelled bitter, like it was a day old by now, and his first sip confirmed it tasted that way, too.

The coffee still reminded him of Amelia.

He dumped the cup in the trash can next to the pay phone that hung in one corner of the diner and pulled out the thick phone book that was stuffed on the shelf below the phone. He paged through the yellow pages, finding the section he wanted. He tore out the first page of law firm listings, pushed the book back on the shelf and left.

Amelia paged through the agreement that Rafe Mendoza had sent with her and read through the paragraphs yet again. The attorney had tried talking her out of some of the stipulations that she'd wanted included, but she'd been adamant.

"You may change your mind," he'd argued. "You want to stay in Texas now, but there's no reason to sign away your choice of moving away later on." His dark eyes had been kind. "You're only twenty-three, Amelia. At least think about it."

"I won't change my mind," she'd told him. But she'd agreed to give it a day and had picked up the agreement that afternoon on her way to the Red Rock regional airport for her return charter to Horseback Hollow.

She closed the document and tucked it back inside the folder Rafe's secretary had provided with the custody agreement and then she climbed out of her aunt's car that she'd borrowed and walked past Quinn's truck toward the house.

It was the middle of the afternoon, so she wasn't particularly surprised when he didn't answer her knock. When she tried the knob and found it locked, though, she was.

A lesson learned from the paparazzi, she assumed with a pang of guilt. Once your privacy was invaded, it was hard to trust that it wouldn't happen again.

Carrying the folder with her, she walked down to the barn and found it empty. There were six horses standing around in the corral next to the barn, their long tails swishing against the heat of the day. She held out her palm over the metal rail and the nearest one nuzzled her palm, obviously looking for a tidbit.

"Sorry, girl," she murmured and rubbed her hand down the horse's white blaze. "Next time I'll bring a treat."

If she'd be allowed a next time.

Following the road with the grassy strip in the center, she kept walking until it began to dip and she could see Quinn's tree house tree in the distance. When she drew closer, she heard the distinctive beat of a hammer.

And even though she'd been gearing herself up for

the past twenty-four hours to see him, her mouth still went dry and her chest tightened.

She tucked the folder under her arm and smoothed back a strand of hair that had worked free from the chignon at her nape. She aimed toward the tree while the hammering grew louder and more distinct, and soon she was standing beneath the shady leaves.

She moved around to where the footholds were and tapped the lowest one with the toe of the Castleton cowboy boots she'd purchased while killing time in Red Rock. Since her whereabouts weren't remotely a secret, she'd also visited Charlene's boutique with her credit card, and stocked up on clothing, including a black silk dress for the Cantina's grand opening. She'd also had lunch with her cousin Wyatt and his wife, Sarah-Jane. And even though Amelia had found Red Rock surprisingly sophisticated and quite lovely, she knew she still preferred the rugged, much smaller Horseback Hollow.

"Fancy boots. You buy them before or after meeting up with that Red Rock lawyer?"

She looked from the detailed stitching over her toe up into the leaves and met Quinn's hazel gaze. "As usual, news is traveling at the speed of light." She ran her palm over the rough tree bark. "Can you come down?"

He swung down from the floor he was constructing and climbed down several footholds before jumping the rest of the way to the ground. He straightened and looked down at her, his expression unreadable. "You going to tell me anything I want to know?"

"I don't know," she said huskily and handed him the folder. "Considering everything that happened last week, you might not welcome anything to do with me."

His lips thinned and he made no attempt to open the

folder. "A hundred reporters camped out on my front porch wouldn't change the fact that you're pregnant with my baby."

"They didn't cause you any more problems, did they?" She tucked her hands in the front pockets of the narrow, black trousers she'd bought at the boutique. There'd been a small selection of delightful maternity clothes, though she hadn't had the nerve to purchase any. Not with the other customers there who'd watched her, somewhat agog, as she'd shopped.

"Guess you'd have seen it on the news if they had." His tone was flat. He gestured with the folder. "You bring this here to settle the fact I can't prevent you from going back to England? Already found that out myself from three different attorneys over in Lubbock."

A pang drove through her. "If that's what you think, you really don't know me at all."

"Saw your earl's press conference."

"Evidently not," she countered, "if you still have the impression that James is *my* anything."

"'Amelia Fortune Chesterfield's support during this difficult time has been steadfast,'" Quinn said, quoting almost verbatim the brief statement that James's staff had released. "'And though we are not betrothed,'" his lips twisted, "'we remain loyal friends.' Didn't exactly say you were never engaged to marry him in the first place."

"People in James's positions don't explain," she said. "They don't complain to the media and they never lend credence to speculation by commenting on anything that smacks of scandal. Which is not to say they won't use the media if it serves their purposes. James's father certainly proved that." She exhaled. "I didn't come here to talk about him." She nodded toward the folder. "I came here to give you that."

Looking even more grim, he flipped open the folder.

His eyes narrowed as he read, his frown coming and going as he flipped slowly through the pages.

"It's a shared custody agreement." Of course he could read for himself what it was, but his silence was more than she could bear. "With stipulations that the baby will bear your name and be raised here in Horseback Hollow."

He finally looked at her. "Why would you do this?"

She lifted her chin. "Why wouldn't I? I've told you more than once I don't want that life." She unconsciously pressed her hand to her abdomen. "I didn't want it for myself and I don't want it for our child. I don't know how else to prove it to you."

"You've already signed it."

"Yes. Duly witnessed by the appropriate individuals." She pressed her tongue to the back of her teeth, hunting for strength. "Go back to your Lubbock attorneys and have them review it. They'll tell you it's exceedingly fair. And once you sign it, there'll be no need for a justice of the peace or a minister."

His jaw canted to one side. He closed the folder and tapped it against the side of his jean-clad thigh. "You *really* don't want to marry me."

"No." She suddenly jabbed her forefinger into his unyielding chest. "*You* really don't want to marry *me*. You're stuck in the past with the one who did betray you. The only reason you want to marry me is to ensure the baby has your name." She gestured at the folder. "Well, happy tidings. Sign it and neither one of us need worry about that a moment longer."

"I don't have a pen."

She felt like her heart was turning to dust inside her chest. She looked up into the leaves above their heads.

He'd build a magical place for their child.

But he wouldn't let himself believe in love.

At least not love with *her*.

"I'm sure you'll find one somewhere," she managed. "You can send me a copy of the agreement once you do."

"And then?"

"And then I guess we'll figure out what to do next." She lifted her hands, feeling helpless. "At least things can't possibly get any worse."

Then she turned on her boot heel and walked away.

Chapter Thirteen

But Amelia was wrong.

Things could get worse.

And they did.

"She is *pregnant?*" Jess's screech could have been heard around the world.

It was certainly enough to wake Quinn from his stupor where he was sprawled on his couch, and he bolted upright, rubbing his hands down his face as his sister stormed into his house brandishing a magazine over her head.

"What?"

She slapped the glossy tabloid on top of Amelia's custody papers that were sitting on the coffee table and picked up the bottle of whiskey he'd tried working his way through the day after Amelia had left him. "Oh, my God." She was clearly disgusted. "You're drunk."

"No. I was drunk." He pinched the bridge of his nose. "Now the term would be *hungover*. So if you'd take your hysterics and leave me the hell alone, I'd appreciate it. And give me back your key to my front door while you're at it."

She sat down on the coffee table in front of him and caught his chin in her hand, giving him a look that was unreasonably similar to their mother's. "You're a grown man who's going to be a father," she tsked. "Start acting like it!"

He brushed her hand aside. The fact that she knew about Amelia's pregnancy was seeping into his throbbing brain. "How'd you find out?"

She shifted and tugged the magazine from under her hip and waved it in front of his face. "Same way everyone on the planet did."

He snatched it from her and stared at the cover of the international tabloid. It contained only a single photograph of a positive pregnancy test stick, with a question mark and the words The Real Cause Behind the End of Jamelia? superimposed over the top.

Disgusted, he threw it aside and shoved off the couch. "Why the *hell* won't everyone just leave her alone!"

Jess narrowed her eyes and studied him. "It's true, then. Amelia is pregnant."

"Whatever happened to people's right to privacy?"

"Privacy's an illusion," Jess said. "I think somebody famous said that. Or the government did. Or—" She shook her head. "Doesn't matter. I'm asking you, Quinn. Is that story true?"

He raked his fingers through his hair. "I didn't read the damn story."

She made a face and straightened. She tilted her head slightly, studying him. "Quinn."

"Yes," he said grudgingly.

"Is it yours?" She quickly lifted her hands peaceably when he glared at her. "I'm just asking!"

"It's mine."

"How do you know? I mean, a week and a half ago, she was supposedly engaged to marry Lord Banning."

"She wouldn't lie to me." His head was clanging and he headed blindly into the kitchen. There was still coffee in the pot from the day before and he dumped it in a mug and drank it cold and stale. Amelia wouldn't lie, yet how many times had he accused her of it, anyway?

Jess had followed him into the kitchen. Her eyes were concerned. "What are you going to do?"

"Not much I can do," he said wearily. "She won't marry me."

His sister's eyebrows disappeared up her forehead. "You, Mr. Never-Get-Married-Again, *proposed?*"

"She refused." More than once and the memory of each time felt engraved on his throbbing brain. He turned on the faucet and stuck his head under the cold water.

When he came up for air, Jess stuck a dish towel in his hand. "Did you tell her you loved her?"

He jerked. "This isn't above love."

"Oh, Quinn." Jess shook her head, looking disgusted all over again. "When it comes to a woman, particularly a pregnant woman, everything is *always* about love."

"Maybe for you." He ran the towel over his face and tossed it aside. "And Mac." His brother-in-law had grown up in Vicker's Corners. "You two've been together since high school. You're the same. Hell, you even teach together at the same school!"

"So? Carrie and you had the same backgrounds, too, and that wasn't exactly a stellar success!"

"There's no comparison between Carrie and Amelia." His voice was abrupt. Carrie had never made him feel half the emotion that Amelia did.

She gave him a look. "Well, duh. It's about time you realized it."

He shoved his fingers through his hair, slicking the wet strands back from his face. He hadn't been talking about the other similarities, despite what his sister obviously thought. "Where'd you see the tabloid?"

"It's front and center on the racks in the Superette."

He exhaled. "This'll send her off the rails." He reached for his Resistol and headed for the door, but his sister grabbed the back of his shirt.

"Hold on there, Romeo," she drawled. "Might want to at least brush your teeth before you go after the fair maiden."

He yanked away. "You're a pain in the ass, you know that?"

"Yeah." She patted his cheek like he was ten. "But nobody loves you like I do. And I kinda fancy the idea of getting some blue blood in our family gene pool." Then she shoved his shoulders, pushing him toward the living room. "And clean clothes wouldn't go amiss, either."

The fact that she was right annoyed the life out of him. He headed toward the steps. "I don't know how Mac puts up with you."

"He loves me," she assured blithely and patted her flat belly. "Which is why we're trying for a girl again." Her eyes were revoltingly merry. "According to that tabloid, your baby and mine will be born right around the same time next January."

Quinn squinted. "You're pregnant, too? Again?"

Jess smiled. "Isn't life grand?"

Amelia stared at the cover of the magazine that her mother had presented the second she'd walked into Aunt Jeanne's house.

The pregnancy stick in the picture was not the same brand Amelia had used either time, but some portion of her mind knew that it didn't really matter.

The message was still the same.

"Well?" Josephine propped her hands on her slender hips and raised her eyebrows. She'd arrived a full day earlier than expected because of the dreadful magazine, and her blue eyes were steely. "Is it true?"

Amelia rubbed her palms down the thighs of her cropped slacks and nodded. Then she gestured at the cover. "I don't know how they found out. Were you contacted for a comment?"

Her mother just gave her a look. "As if we would have offered one to such a disreputable publication? My senior social secretary gave me a copy when no one else on my staff seemed to have the nerve to show it to me." She sighed and sat down on the couch next to her. They were alone in the house only because Jeanne Marie and Deke had gone to see Toby and his crew for a while. "We'll have to release something officially at some point, but I wanted to see you for myself, first. Darling, why didn't you *tell* me?"

Amelia's throat tightened. "I was going to. I just wanted to clean up some of the mess I made after the whole Jamelia business exploded."

Her mother closed her cool hands around Amelia's

and squeezed gently. "Are you feeling all right? I hate knowing you've been dealing with this all on your own."

"It's about time I finally dealt with something on my own," she murmured thickly. She met her mother's eyes. "I'm sorry I've done such a poor job of it."

"Amelia." Josephine sighed. "I love you. The only thing I am concerned about is that you're happy. I knew you weren't happy in London even before this ridiculous betrothal business with James came about." She tucked Amelia's hair behind her ear the same way she'd been doing since Amelia was a tot. "Had you confided in me, perhaps we could have prevented some of this outrageous publicity."

Amelia chewed the inside of her cheek. "Molly knew," she whispered. "She's the only one other than Quinn who knew I was pregnant."

Josephine's expression cooled. "*My* Molly?"

Amelia nodded miserably. "I don't want to believe she would have said something, but who else was there?" James hadn't known she was returning to Horseback Hollow, much less that she was pregnant with Quinn's baby, so the information couldn't have come from his quarter.

"And your Quinn," Josephine said gently. "He wouldn't have—"

"No." Amelia shook her head, adamant. He might have threatened that one time to out her pregnancy during Jeanne Marie's and Deke's family dinner, but he never would have gone beyond that. Certainly not to the very type of strangers he'd threatened off the Rocking-U. She reached for the hateful tabloid and flipped it open to the main article that turned out to be only a few paragraphs, accompanied by two pages of photographs obviously meant to chronicle the rise and fall of her and James's supposed romance.

There were also a startling number of images of Quinn that had to have taken some effort to collect. One was even of him as a solemn boy, standing next to an easily recognizable Jess and a woman she could only assume was their mother, given the casket they were looking at. She trailed her fingertip over his young face then made herself look at the text.

"'Sources close to Amelia Fortune Chesterfield and her baby daddy, Horseback Hollow Homewrecker Quinn Drummond, confirm that the stick turned a big, positive blue,'" she read aloud. Then she made a face and flipped the magazine closed, tossing it aside. "Ophelia Malone finally gets her big payday," she muttered. "And Quinn didn't do a thing to deserve her trashy comments."

"I'll have to deal with Molly." Josephine rose and paced around the parlor. Her silver hair was immaculately coiffed and despite her day of travel, she looked impeccable in a black and white pantsuit. "I'll have Jensen look into her finances." She referred to Amelia's third-eldest brother. "If there's proof she was compensated, we can take her to court since it's a violation of her confidentiality agreement. Jensen knows how to be discreet."

"Whereas I don't."

Her mother sent her an exasperated look. "Stop reading between the lines, Amelia. I wasn't implying any such thing."

"I want it all to go away." She twisted her hands together. "You always said if we ignored rumors and gossip, they'll die of starvation."

"Well, that used to be truer than it is nowadays. People don't depend on news to come from reputable news-papers and the nightly news." She sighed. "It's become quite exhausting in the past few years." She brushed her hand down her silk sleeve. "Either that, or I'm just getting too old to want to put up with it."

"You're not old, Mum."

Josephine's lips twisted a little. "I'm sixty-two, darling. I've divorced one husband and buried another. Now I'm going to be a grandmamma again, and maybe I would like to slow down my schedule and enjoy that more this time around than I was able to do with Oliver Junior."

She sat down beside Amelia again and hugged her arm around her shoulders. "I don't want you worrying about Molly. She's my secretary and I'll see that matter is handled appropriately. In the meantime, you can tell me more about your Mr. Drummond."

Amelia's nose burned. "Quinn is anything but *my* Mr. Drummond," she said thickly.

"Do you love him?"

Amelia nodded. "I knew he was special the first time I saw him. When we were here for Sawyer's wedding. Remember?"

"I remember."

"I couldn't get him out of my head. When I came for Toby's wedding, I made the excuse that I just wanted some space from James pressuring me about marrying, but I had to see Quinn again."

Her mother smiled softly. She rested her head against Amelia's. "I felt the same way the first time I saw your father."

Tears collected and squeezed out her eyes. "He'd be so ashamed of me," Amelia whispered.

Josephine tsked. "He'd have been ready to put Quinn's head on a spike," she allowed, gently teasing. "Because you were his baby girl. But then he'd have come to his senses, the way Simon always did, and start campaigning for the baby to be named after him."

Amelia smiled through her tears. "Yes." She wrapped her arms around her mother's neck. "Yes, he would have. I love you, Mum."

"I love you too, darling." Josephine squeezed her back. "And everything is going to be all right. You'll see."

They both heard the crunch of tires from outside and Josephine stood again while Amelia swiped her cheeks. "Sounds like my sister and Deke are back already. I hope they have good news finally about Toby and Angie's adoption."

Only it quickly became apparent that it wasn't Amelia's aunt and uncle, when her mother looked out the window. "Oh, my." She turned and eyed Amelia for a moment, then picked up her suitcase that was still sitting near the front door where she'd left it upon arriving. "I'm going to go upstairs and get settled."

Amelia started to tell her that she was using the room her mother was accustomed to, but broke off when she spotted Quinn crossing in front of the window.

A moment later, he was pounding on the front door. "Open up, Amelia," he said loudly. "I saw you sitting in there."

She nervously tucked her hair behind her ears and moved to the door, waiting until her mother was gone before tugging it open.

His hazel eyes were bloodshot and they raked over her face. "Was that your mother I saw?"

She nodded. "She's a day earlier than I expected," she said inanely.

He brushed past her, entering the house even though she hadn't exactly issued an invitation. "Are you all right?"

He was looking at the magazine lying on the coffee table.

Dismay sank through her belly and her shoulders bowed. "You've seen it." She could tell by the lack of shock on his face.

"Jess brought a copy by."

"I'm sorry," she said huskily. "If I would have just stayed in London, you would never have been dragged into any of this."

"And I wouldn't know you're having my baby." His voice was flat. "Regretting the papers you had drawn up already?"

"No!" She lifted her hands. "I don't know what else to do, Quinn." She waved at the tabloid. "Thanks to that nastiness, every last bit of privacy we might have had is lost."

"I don't give a rip who knows about us," he said impatiently. "But I also don't want you working yourself up into a state over it."

Her lips parted. "You were worried about me?"

His gaze raked over her again. "That's my baby you're carrying. You think I want anything endangering that?"

She pressed her lips together, her hopes sinking yet again. Of course his concern would be for the baby. "As you can see, I'm fine."

"Suppose your mother wants to take you back."

"Actually, no." Her voice cooled even more. "I've

made it more than clear to you that I intend to remain in Horseback Hollow and raise our child here where he—"

"She—"

"—will have both parents in his life." She stepped closer to him, looking up into his face. She'd seen him just the day before when she'd left him the agreement, but he looked like he hadn't slept in weeks. "Why are you so insistent that the baby is a girl?"

He picked up the magazine and flipped it open to the article. "Got enough boys in the family," he muttered. "Little girl would be a change of pace."

Her throat tightened. How easy it was to imagine him holding a baby girl. Their child would succeed in wrapping him around a tiny finger.

He would love the baby. He just wouldn't love her.

She rubbed her damp palms down her thighs again, banishing the image before she started crying like a baby herself. "Did you consult an attorney about the, uh, the agreement?"

He tossed the magazine down again. "I don't need to consult anyone. And I haven't signed it."

"Why not? It gives you everything you wanted!"

His lips twisted. "You'd think."

Her head felt light in a way that it hadn't since she'd first arrived in Horseback Hollow. She thought about how many times he'd seemed stuck on the idea that she'd be happier back in London. "Do you *want* me to go back to London?"

His brows pulled together. "No."

Her hands lifted, palms upward. "Then what, Quinn?"

"I want to know I can protect you from crap like that!" He gestured at the magazine. "And I know I can't."

Her heart squeezed and she had to remind herself that

feeling protective wasn't the same thing as feeling love. "I wanted to protect you, too," she said huskily. "And I didn't do a good job of it, either. I confided in Molly—" She broke off and shook her head. "I shouldn't have trusted anyone but my own family. And you."

"You know for sure it was her?"

"Who else?" She sat down on the arm of the couch and held her arms tightly around her chest. "You said nobody saw you buy the test kit I used here. I know you didn't tell anyone. That just leaves Molly. You think you trust someone and they betray—" She broke off. "I don't want to think about it anymore." She watched him for a moment. "I thought I'd, um, speak with Christopher about volunteering at the Fortune Foundation office once he gets it up and running here. I could offer music lessons or something."

"Thought you didn't like playing in front of people."

"I don't like performing. But one-on-one? I told you once I liked working with children." She wished she wouldn't have brought it up, because it only made her remember that perfect April night when she'd talked about her life and he'd actually seemed to listen. "I...I have to do something to fill my days."

"You'll have a baby to fill your days." He waited a beat. "Or are you planning to hire some nanny to do that? That's what people like you do, right?"

"People like you," she repeated, mimicking his drawl. "I was born into a family that happened to have money," she said crisply. "It doesn't make me a different species than you!"

His jaw flexed. "People with your financial advantage," he refined. "That's what my dad's father's *real* family did. Hired...nannies."

She studied the fresh lines creasing his tanned forehead. He'd said his father was illegitimate but hadn't offered anything else about it. Only had used it as a reason why she ought to marry him. "What do you mean?"

"Baxter Anthony." He practically spit the name. "My grandfather. He had a wife. He had kids. His *real* family. The ones who lived in comfort on a big old ranch in Oklahoma. While my grandmother—whom he fired as one of those nannies after knocking her up—and my dad eked out a life in Horseback Hollow. Baxter's real family had nannies. They had private schools. They had everything that my old man didn't."

"I don't want a nanny," she said after a moment. "It never even entered my mind. But the baby won't be here for months yet, and I'm not exactly used to sitting around, whiling away my days waving a lacy fan and eating bonbons."

"You could use a few bonbons," he muttered. "You're still too thin."

"Gawky, skinny Amelia." She sighed. "Lucie got all the grace in the family."

"What the hell are you talking about?"

She shrugged dismissively. "It doesn't matter."

"You're the most graceful thing I've ever seen," he said in such a flat tone she couldn't possibly mistake it for a compliment. More like an accusation. "You're so far out of my league it's laughable. I still can't believe you danced with me that night, much less—" He broke off and shoveled his fingers through his hair, leaving the thick brown strands disheveled.

She tucked her tongue between her teeth, trying to make sense of his words. "You're the one who seemed out of reach to me," she finally said. Self-assured. Quietly confident. A man who'd held her and made her feel safe and beautiful and wanted.

His brows were pulled down, his eyes unreadable. "Baxter was the only one who wanted to buy the Rocking-U when my old man died." His lips thinned. "He'd buy it now, too, if I'd let him. Just so he could finally succeed in wiping away the evidence that anyone with his blood ever existed here."

"Forget about him! The man sounds hideous. And why would you want to sell the Rocking-U? That ranch is—" She broke off, trying to make sense of the nonsensical. "It's who you are," she finally finished and knew she had it right. Ranching wasn't merely something Quinn did. It was entwined with everything he was. The ranch was an extension of him just as much as he was an extension of it.

"It's the only way I can bring something equal to the table," he said through his teeth.

She pushed to her feet. "Let me get this straight," she said slowly. "You think the only thing you can offer this baby is *money?*" She laughed, but it sounded more hysterical than anything. "Money doesn't matter, Quinn! Good Lord, how can you think it would?"

"Because you've always had it," he said roughly.

"If I gave it all away would that make you happy?" Her voice rose. "Would that soothe your...your *ego?*" She swept out her arms, taking in the room around them. "How can you stand in this home that *love* so obviously built and talk that way?"

She snatched up the tabloid and threw it at his chest. "You should have sold the story," she said icily. "At least then you would have been the one to make a fortune on it. You know what? *Don't* sign the custody agreement.

I'd rather take this baby back to London than have him be raised by a man who can't recognize what's right in front of his face!"

Then, because tears were blinding her and her stomach was heaving, she fled upstairs.

Quinn started after her. She'd walked away the other day when she brought him that custody agreement and he wasn't going to let her walk off again.

He got to the top of the stairs just as she slammed the bathroom door shut and he started to reach for it.

"I would give her a little time," a calm voice said.

He looked from Amelia's mother, standing in a bedroom doorway, to the bathroom door. On the other side, he could hear Amelia retching, and his sense of helplessness made him want to punch a wall.

"Come." Lady Josephine walked toward him and tucked her hand around his arm, drawing him away from the door. "No woman wants to be overheard when they're in Amelia's state. Morning sickness is never fun." She smiled at him with unexpected kindness.

But he also noticed the way she subtly placed herself between him and the door.

"She's in there because of me." He wasn't only talking about her pregnancy. "She's upset."

"Yes." Lady Josephine's expression didn't change. Nor did her protective position or the steel behind her light touch on his arm. "It's been upsetting business. Come."

He reluctantly went with her back down the stairs and followed her into the parlor. She glanced out the window, then sat on the edge of a side chair, her hands folded in her lap, her long legs angled to one side. It was such an "Amelia position" that he had to look away.

"Mr. Drummond, please sit."

He exhaled and feeling like a kid called in front of the principal, sat on one end of the couch. "Call me Quinn. Lady Josephine," he tacked on hurriedly. Was it supposed to be Lady Chesterfield? Lady Fortune Chesterfield? He wished to hell he'd listened more to Jess's yammering about all that.

A faint smile was playing around the corners of the woman's lips. "And you may call me Josephine. We are a bit of family after all."

He could feel heat rising up his neck. "I suppose I should apologize for that. I wouldn't blame you if you wanted my head."

Her head tilted slightly. "Are you saying you took advantage of my daughter?" Before he could answer, she shifted slightly. "Amelia has a kind heart," she said. "She's always hated the attention our family is given back home. As if we're celebrities of some sort. Unfortunately, this business with Lord Banning got quite out of control and in hindsight, I wish I would have interfered early on. Perhaps I could have saved us all some of this embarrassment. But I've actually never witnessed Amelia allowing herself to be taken advantage of. In fact, she can be quite headstrong at times." Her blue gaze didn't allow him to look away. "I feel certain she was an equal participant in this situation."

"Lady—"

"Josephine."

"Josephine." He rubbed his hands down his jeans and stood, because just sitting there had his nerves wanting to jump out of his skin. "No disrespect, ma'am, but I'm not going to talk about that." He wasn't going to talk about having sex with Amelia to her mother. He wasn't going to talk about it with anyone.

"I've always thought that when two people who belong together are not, it's one of the saddest things there is."

He stared. "You think she belongs with *me*. I'm a small-town rancher, ma'am. I don't have a pot of gold. I've got one failed marriage and pots of cow manure."

Her lips twitched. "I forget how refreshingly frank you Americans can be." She rose gracefully. She was taller than Amelia, but no less slender, and Quinn knew when Amelia was her age, she'd be just as beautiful. "I had an unsuccessful marriage as well, Quinn. And then I met Amelia's father and I had a very, very successful one. I loved Simon with all of my heart and knew that he loved me equally. I want that for Amelia. I want that for all of my children. The past is past. And if you'll forgive an unintended pun, fortune isn't in gold. I hope you'll realize that for both your sakes."

She patted his arm as she passed him and pulled open the front door. "You don't have to love Amelia to be a good father to your child together. But if you don't love Amelia, be decent enough to allow her space to find someone who will."

Chapter Fourteen

"Come on." Jess dragged Quinn by the arm, pulling him toward the brightly lit building.

The Hollows Cantina was having its grand opening celebration and everyone in town seemed to have turned out for the festivities.

"Mac reserved a table for us," Jess continued, "and is waiting, and you are *not* getting out of coming just because you're a flaming idiot."

"Amelia's going to be there."

"No kidding, Sherlock." She dug her fingernails into his forearm the same way she'd done when she was an equally irritating teenager. "Maybe if you weren't so clueless when it comes to wooing a woman, you'd be with her instead of playing third wheel to me and my husband."

"I don't want to be here with you, either," he reminded. But she'd driven out to the Rocking-U and made it plain she wasn't leaving unless he came with her.

For the sake of a little peace and sanity, and only because he really didn't want to upset yet another pregnant woman, he had pulled on the only suit he owned and gone with her.

"I'll be just as happy to go back home again," he finished. There were strands of white lights strung around the Cantina's building, outlining not only the second story's open-air terrace, but the market umbrellas lining the street in front of it, and country music spewed out from inside. The festive atmosphere was the last thing he was in the mood for.

"Over my dead body," Jess raised her voice over the music and even though there were a couple dozen people lined up outside the entrance waiting to get in, she pulled him into the throng, waving at the familiar faces they passed. He knew everyone in Horseback Hollow, too, but she knew everyone from Vicker's Corners who was there as well, which made for slow going. But they finally reached the small table deep inside the first floor of the restaurant where Mac was already seated.

She slipped behind the table to sit next to her husband who shoved out the chair that had obviously been added to what should have been a two-person table for Quinn. He gestured with his half-empty beer mug. "Place is a madhouse," he said, leaning across the table so he could be heard above the noise. "Already put in orders for a beer for you."

Jess made a face and reached for her glass of fruit juice. "Some men might forgo alcohol in support of his pregnant wife having to abstain."

Mac grinned at her, obviously unfazed. "Baby, you're

pregnant so often, I'd never have another beer again if I gave it up whenever you're knocked up." He bussed her cheek. "I ordered you some hot crab dip," he added. "You can eat yourself silly on it."

Jess looked slightly mollified. "At least I know I won't have to share it with either one of you." Both Mac and Quinn detested crab. "You wouldn't know there had ever been any protests in town about this place opening." She was craning her neck around, openly gawking at the people crowded inside. "This is amazing!" She wriggled a little in her seat, clearly delighted. "I think every person from Horseback Hollow *and* Vicker's Corners must be here tonight."

Quinn was looking around, too, hopefully less noticeably than his sister.

But he hadn't spotted Amelia.

He knew she hadn't left town. Jess would've reported it.

A waitress wearing a stark white blouse and a black apron tied around her hips stopped next to their table and delivered a steaming crock of crab dip and crackers as well as two freshly frosted mugs filled with beer. "We have a special menu tonight," she told them as she dealt three one-page menus on the table. "Because of the grand openin' and all. I'll give you a chance to look it over and be back if you have any questions."

Quinn's only question was where Amelia was.

Not that he knew what he would say to her if he saw her. She was making a habit of walking away from him. The fact that he deserved it wasn't something he was willing to look at real closely.

And he was still feeling the bruises from her mother's velvet-over-steel dismissal the day before.

He lifted the beer mug, and angled in his seat so he could see around the restaurant more easily.

The staircase that led to the second floor was situated close to the center of the room; a wide iron and rustic wood thing that was as much a focal point as it was functional and the mayor, Harlan Osgood, was holding court at the base, recounting the steps taken to bring such a fine establishment to their little town as if he hadn't ever had his own doubts about it. Privately, Quinn figured it was a good thing Harlan's main job was as the town's barber, because a natural politician, he wasn't.

Marcos and Wendy Mendoza, the owners, were working the room, too. The young couple was eye-catching, to say the least. Wendy in particular looked more like she belonged on the cover of magazines than making the desserts that Julia claimed were out of this world. Quinn had to give the couple credit for seeming to give equal attention to everyone they stopped to speak with. They gave just as much time to Tanya and her folks, sitting at a table as crowded as Quinn's across the room, as they did the mayor.

"Mac, what are you going to have?" Jess was asking, tapping the crisp edge of her menu against the table. "I'm starving. I haven't had a speck of morning sickness in two days, and I am going to take advantage of it."

Mac chuckled. "I think I'm having whatever else it is you want to order so you can eat it, too."

Was Amelia still plagued with morning sickness?

Quinn pushed out of the chair.

Jess looked at him. "You're *not* leaving."

He leaned over her. "Stop bossing," he warned.

Then he kissed the top of her head and made his way toward the staircase. He knew the entire extended Fortune family was supposed to be there that night, and if they weren't on the bottom floor, maybe they were up top.

Getting there proved as slow-going as getting into the restaurant in the first place, though, because of all the people standing around on the stairs blocking the way. He could hear bursts of laughter coming from the upper floor and barely controlled the urge to physically move some of the roadblocks out of his way.

"Mr. Drummond!"

He looked over the side of the staircase to see Shayla waving at him excitedly, her orange ponytail bouncing, and he sketched a wave. But she was already worming her way around the mayor and up the steps until she was only a few below his position midway up. "It's so cool to see you," she gushed. "Is Lady Amelia here, too?"

The girl had helped them avoid Ophelia Malone in Vicker's Corners, so Quinn swallowed his impatience to get upstairs. "I'm looking for her now," he admitted. "How've you been? Do you still have a particular guest staying at the B and B?"

She widened her eyes dramatically. "Right? Miz Malone finally left this morning. My ma's not so happy—" she waved her hand behind her, presumably to indicate the presence of her mother somewhere in the madhouse "—'cause she paid the room on time and all, but I was glad to see her go. I can't believe what she got printed the other day." She wrinkled her nose. "So gross."

It was as good a definition as any and a lot milder than what Quinn still thought about the tabloid cover. "Did you and your mom already have dinner?"

"Nah. Not yet." She twisted her head around, looking

down on the patrons below. "Ma's over there talking to the Fremonts. They're all on the graduation committee for high school next year."

He automatically glanced over at the table he'd noticed earlier where Tanya sat with her parents. Shayla's mother's hair was just as orange as her daughter's. Either the color was real or they shared the same bottle of hair dye.

"Can't believe she did it," Shayla was babbling on. "Just so stupid, you know?"

He frowned. "What?"

"Tanya." Shayla rolled her eyes, looking disgusted. "Believe me, she's not one of *my* friends anymore."

God save him from teenage girl angst. He managed to edge up another step when the person in front of him moved slightly. "That's too bad," he said vaguely. Tanya had always been a hard worker for him and the dozen or so other people she also cleaned for in order to help supplement her family's strained income.

"Wow. You're nicer than I would be," Shayla was saying. She was practically shouting to be heard above the music. "Blabbing about your personal business to Miz Malone and all."

He went still, her words penetrating.

He went back down the step. "What did you say?"

Shayla looked suddenly nervous. "Uh—"

He nudged her to one side of the stairs so one of the servers carrying a stack of menus could get past them. "What do you mean about personal business, Shayla?" But he had the sinking feeling he already knew.

He'd tossed Amelia's pregnancy test in the trash.

Tanya cleaned his house.

Shayla shot a look toward the table below and Quinn

caught the pale expression on Tanya's face even from a distance.

"I don't think she meant to," Shayla said hurriedly. She might be willing to eschew Tanya's friendship, but she was obviously afraid of tossing her under the bus. "It's just Miz Malone kept talking to everybody and... and—" She lifted her shoulders. "Well, Tanya needed that car in the worst way or she's not gonna be able to get back and forth to Lubbock for school when she graduates next year and the money she gets cleaning houses is already used up on her ma's medicine. I thought you already knew."

Quinn sucked down his fury.

"I don't think she knew how bad it would be," Shayla finished. "Still." She made a face. "*I* wouldn't want her cleaning around my stuff. You're prob'ly pretty mad, huh."

Amelia's friend Molly hadn't done a single thing to betray her.

"It's okay, Shayla." He squeezed her shoulder and managed a smile even though he wanted to kick both Ophelia Malone and Tanya Fremont off the planet altogether. "I'm glad to hear the truth."

"Quinn!"

He looked toward the top of the stairs to see Liam beckoning.

"Go on and enjoy your dinner," Quinn told Shayla. "Once I find Amelia, I'll let her know you're here. I'm sure she'll want to say hello."

Shayla beamed. "You think?"

He nodded and started edging up the stairs again while she slipped through the people on her way down.

Liam clapped him on the shoulder when he finally

made it to the top. "Julia's done a helluva job here to-night with the Mendozas, hasn't she?" The man's face was proud. "We've got the whole family up here."

Suspicions confirmed, Quinn looked beyond Liam to the crowded tables spilling out onto the open terrace. Jeanne and Deke were sitting with Josephine and their brother, James Marshall Fortune. There was also another older couple sitting with them and he was pretty certain the man was the threesome's older brother, John. Which, according to Jess who always needed to know who was who, made him Wendy Mendoza's father. Aside from Jeanne and Deke's crew, spread out among the rest of the tables were a bunch of other faces he recognized from Sawyer and Laurel's New Year's wedding.

But Amelia was not among them.

"We've got extra reason to celebrate," Liam was saying. "Angie and Toby's adoption was finally approved."

His head was still banging with Shayla's news, but Quinn glanced at the man who seemed deep in conversation with his uncle James. Happiness radiated from his face. "That's great," he said. "Where's Amelia?"

Liam looked surprised for a moment, then glanced around. "Don't know, man. She was here earlier." He raised his voice even more. "Aunt Josephine, where'd Amelia go?"

In addition to Amelia's mother, Quinn suddenly found himself the focus of way too many eyes.

Josephine said something to her companions, then rose and worked her way through the tables toward him.

"I didn't mean to interrupt your dinner," Quinn said.

"You're not interrupting," she assured. She smiled slightly at her nephew. "Liam, I haven't had a chance yet to applaud your fiancée's efforts tonight. Is Julia going to be able to join us, or is she on duty all evening?"

"She's not on duty at all," Liam said, grinning. "But she can't keep from checking on things. She'll be 'round soon enough." He headed after the waitress that was circulating throughout the room with a tray laden with drinks. "Hey there, darlin', lemme take one of those off your hands."

Josephine looked back at Quinn. "I wasn't sure we would have the pleasure of seeing you tonight."

He wondered what she'd really like to say if she weren't so polite. Probably something more along the lines of hoping he wouldn't have the gall to show his face that night.

"I wasn't going to come," he admitted. He was glad he had, though, if only to hear what Shayla'd had to say. "Is Amelia all right?"

Josephine's expression was the same as it had been the other day when she'd essentially told him to put up or shut up. Calm. Seemingly gracious, yet still reserved.

"She's unhappy." She didn't attempt to raise her voice above the music to be heard, yet her words somehow managed to carry through anyway. "As are you, I believe." Then she sighed a little, her gaze following Sawyer and Orlando Mendoza as they moved among the tables. "I keep having to remind myself how entwined the Fortune and Mendoza families are," she murmured then looked back at Quinn again. "She went outside a short while ago. She said she needed some fresh air."

He stifled an oath. How had he missed her leaving the restaurant when he'd been on the damn stairs?

"Thank you." He started to turn and go back the way he'd come, but stopped. "La— Josephine."

She lifted her eyebrows, waiting.

"It wasn't Molly," he said abruptly. "You know. Who spilled the beans." He told her briefly about Tanya cleaning his place.

When he was done, he couldn't tell if she was relieved or not. He'd thought that Amelia's "royal face" was bad, but in comparison to her mother's, her expressive face was an open book.

"What do you plan to do about your young employee?"

"Fire her," he said flatly.

"Hmm." She nodded once. "Is that why you're anxious to see my daughter? To share this information?"

He could lie and say it was, even though he'd been looking for Amelia before Shayla's disclosure. As far as he was concerned, what went on between him and Amelia *was* between him and Amelia. "I don't know why I'm anxious to see her," he finally said truthfully. "I just know I have to."

It wasn't any sort of answer, but it seemed enough for her to smile just a little as she nodded once and headed back to her table.

He went down the stairs again where the sounds of celebration weren't as raucous, though the music was, and pretended he didn't see his sister trying to flag him down as he worked his way toward the entrance.

Once he got past the crowd still waiting to get in, he felt like he'd been shot from a noisy cannon into blissful peace.

The music was still loud. There were still dozens of people surrounding the tables beneath the colorful market umbrellas. But it was still *open* and he yanked off his suit jacket and hauled in a deep breath of fresh air.

The Hollows Cantina might well be bringing new jobs and new revenue to the area, and it wouldn't be crazy busy in the days to come like it was for the grand opening, but he was pretty sure he wouldn't be in any hurry to go back, no matter how good the food might turn out to be.

Bunching his jacket in one hand, he scanned the tables outside the restaurant. Amelia wasn't at any of them, so he walked past them until he reached the side of the building. She wasn't there, either, so he walked all the way around the building. And even then, he didn't spot her.

"Dammit, Amelia. Where are you?"

The whole of Horseback Hollow's businesses were contained in just a few short blocks and trying not to imagine her passed out cold in some shadowy corner, he started down the street, and then nearly missed her altogether where she was sitting on a bench in front of the mayor's barbershop.

The soles of his boots scraped against the street when he stopped in front of her and peered at her in the dark. Her skin looked white in the moonlight, her hair, eyes and clothing as dark as midnight. "You're not easy to find."

"I didn't know you were looking." She shifted slightly, given away only by the slight rustle of her clothes. "You've been in the restaurant?"

"Yeah." It was a warm night and he tossed his jacket on the bench beside her and started rolling up his sleeves. "It's a zoo."

She made a soft sound. "Yes. Too many people and too much noise for me."

"Were you feeling sick?"

She shifted again. "Not in the way you mean," she murmured. "What do you want, Quinn?"

"Molly didn't rat us out," he said abruptly. "It was Tanya. When she cleaned the house—"

"She found the test," Amelia finished slowly, dawning revelation clear in her tone. "Of course she did. I can't believe I never thought of that."

"I can't believe she talked to that woman," he said flatly. "I wouldn't have known if Shayla hadn't said something. Would've just kept paying the kid every Sunday to clean the bathrooms and mop the damn floors, never knowing any better."

"She's a girl," Amelia murmured.

"She talked about *our* business for the price of a car," he countered. "She won't be stepping foot in my house again. Or any others, if I can help it."

"Didn't you ever make a mistake when you were young?"

His lips twisted. "Why are you being so understanding? You were pretty upset thinking it was your mother's secretary."

"It's just all so…so sad, isn't it?" Her voice was soft. Oddly musing. "I'd say it was tragic except there are so many other real tragedies occurring every day." She sighed. "The press has been vilifying us ever since I came to Horseback Hollow. Ophelia used Tanya like a tool, no differently than she'd use a long-distance lens. Have you ever noticed how random it all is?" she asked abruptly.

He peered at her face but even though his eyes were becoming accustomed to the dark, he still couldn't tell if she was looking at him or not. "What's random?"

"If I hadn't decided to come to Horseback Hollow

with Mum for Sawyer's wedding over New Year's. If you and I hadn't danced when I came back again for Toby's. If James's father hadn't announced an engagement-that-wasn't. If any one of those things hadn't occurred, everything would be so different today."

"Maybe that's not random." His chest felt tight. "Maybe that's fate."

She shifted, her dark dress rustling. "You believe in fate." She sounded skeptical.

"I don't know what I believe, Amelia. Except I know I don't want you going back to London."

"I've told you and told you, you needn't worry about your place in the baby's life."

"What about a place in your life?"

She went silent for a moment, then slowly stood, walking closer to him until he could smell the clean fragrance of her hair and see the gleam in her dark eyes.

"Did you really want me to come back to Horseback Hollow after the night we shared? You said you did. And I…I thought you meant it. But maybe that's just what a person is supposed to say after a one-night stand. Protocol, if you will."

"It wasn't protocol," he said flatly. "I meant it."

He felt the weight of her gaze. "Why?"

The shirt button he'd left loose at his neck wasn't enough and he yanked another one free. "What d'ya mean *why?* I liked you. We had great—"

"Sex," she finished.

"*Chemistry* is what I was going to say."

"The end result is the same."

"Where are you going with this, Amelia?"

"I don't know." She sighed. "I've just been trying to

figure out how much I imagined about that night and what was actually real."

He didn't need light. He closed one arm around her waist and pressed his other hand against her flat abdomen, feeling as much as hearing the sudden breath she inhaled. "That is real."

"Yes." The one word sounded shaky. "But sex is not love. Having a baby doesn't mean love, either."

"Sometimes it does." He wanted to get out the words. But they felt stopped in his chest by a lifetime of disappointments. "Jess and Mac are having another baby. Trying again for a girl. So maybe she really had been in that hardware store to buy pink paint."

"I'm happy for them." Her voice was low. She gently patted his chest once. Then once more. "Think about it before you fire Tanya," she murmured. And then she stepped out of his arm and started up the street, disappearing into the dark.

Chapter Fifteen

Amelia's eyes glazed as she stumbled up the street.

"Amelia!"

Quinn was not going to come around. He wouldn't let himself, and she couldn't bear it.

"Don't walk away from me."

Her chest ached. She'd never understood that a heart breaking was a physical breaking, too. She could barely force herself to move when all she wanted to do was curl into a ball. She swiped her cheek and forced her feet to move faster. "What are you going to do? Throw me over your shoulder?"

"Please." Just one word. Rough. And raw.

Her feet dragged to a stop.

A block away, she could see the lights of the Cantina. Could hear the music playing on the night.

She didn't have to look back to see Quinn coming up

behind her. She didn't even need to hear his footfalls on the pavement. She could feel him.

"Toby and Angie's adoption was approved this afternoon. Did you know that?"

"Yeah. I saw him and your uncle James together. D'you think he's the one who gave him that money?"

"Aunt Jeanne wouldn't take the money he wanted to give her, so why not? He can afford it." She clasped her arms around her waist, trying to keep the pieces of herself from splintering on the road and nodded toward the festivities. "Everyone in there is celebrating," she said painfully. "Everyone in there is happy. Julia and Liam can walk into a room and light it up simply by looking at each other. Colton and Stacey are like two halves of a whole. I think Jude would lay down his life for Gabi and Christopher and Kinsley—" Her voice broke. "They're all happy. They're all in love. Is it so wrong to want that, too?"

"No."

She turned on her heel and looked up at him. "I could marry you, Quinn," she whispered. "Justice of the peace or a minister. It wouldn't matter. I could stand up in front of either and promise to love you for the rest of my days. And I wouldn't be lying." She sniffed but the tears kept coming. "But the marriage *would* be a lie, because I know you don't love me. And I can't live like that." She turned again, desperate to go somewhere, anywhere, for a little peace.

"And I can't live without you."

Had she gone so far over the edge that she was hearing things now, too?

"Don't leave me."

She sucked in a shuddering breath.

"Amelia." He closed his hands over her shoulders and turned her toward him. "Please." His low voice cracked. "Don't leave me." His fingers tightened, almost painfully.

"Quinn—"

He closed his mouth over hers, his hands moving to cradle her face. "Don't," he said hoarsely, brushing his thumbs over her cheeks. "I can take anything but that."

She could no more stop her hands from grasping his shoulders than she could stop loving him.

He kissed her again, lightly. Tenderly. The way he had that very first time. "If you leave me, I won't be able to take it. I love you," he whispered. "More than I've ever loved anything or anyone. And I am terrified. Okay?"

She wound her arms behind his neck, her heart cracking wide. "Nothing terrifies you."

"Not being good enough for you does." He dragged her arms away, holding them captive between them. "Not being a good enough father." He shook her gently, as if trying to convince her. "Not being a good enough husband. If I failed you or the baby—"

"You won't," she cried. "You can't fail me if you'd just love me. You think I'm not afraid? I don't even know how to make a baby's bottle. Infants can't eat peanut butter sandwiches!"

He folded her against him, tucking her head into his shoulder. "I know how to make a bottle," he said roughly. "Jess made me learn years ago. That's the easy stuff, Amelia. I'm talking about a life. What do I have to offer you?"

"Your heart," she said thickly. "Offer your heart! It's the only thing that matters. If you're afraid, be afraid with me. I can't bear it if you shut me out."

"Oh, my God," a voice said from nearby, startling them both. "Get a room or get on with it."

Amelia stared into the darkness, appalled when Ophelia Malone strolled closer. All of her pain, her uncertainty where Quinn was concerned, coalesced into a ball of hatred toward the paparazzo. *"You."* She started to launch herself at the dreadful woman, but Quinn held her back. "Haven't you done enough?"

"Evidently not." Ophelia sighed slightly. She held out her hands to her sides and Amelia spotted the camera she was holding.

She pulled against Quinn, but again he held fast. "She's not worth it." His voice was cutting.

"Why do you do this?" Amelia demanded of the woman. "Why do you go around making peoples' lives a misery? Is the money that good? Is it just that you enjoy tearing people's lives to shreds? What is it?"

"Oh, the money was good. Very, very good. But it didn't work anyway." Ophelia circled around them, giving Amelia's clawed fingers a wide berth. "Even knowing what sort of person you really are, Lord Banning *still* isn't giving my sister a chance."

Amelia shook her head, suddenly lost. "What?"

Ophelia sighed again. "You really are as dumb as a post," she mocked. "Your rancher there has more smarts than you do. At least he built that successful little ranch of his out of nothing but ashes. What have you ever done but smile pretty for the cameras while your mummy does all that charitable work that has people thinking she's such a saint?"

Quinn set Amelia to one side of him and snatched Ophelia's wrist with his free hand, making the other woman drop the camera. "Keep it up," he spat, "and I'll let her at you."

"Who's your sister?"

Ophelia shook off Quinn's hold and crouched down to pick up the two pieces of the camera. She held up the lens to the light from the Cantina, then tossed it off to the side of the road. "So much for that pricey little thing." She pushed to her feet. "Astrid," she clipped. She circled around Quinn until she was near Amelia again. "Astrid is my sister and if it weren't for *you* and your eminently suitable pedigree, Lord Banning would have chosen *her*. He would have gone against that decrepit father of his and married my sister whether she was a common shop girl or not!"

"You're insane," Amelia whispered, shocked to her very core.

Ophelia held out her arms. "Guilty as charged, no doubt." She suddenly tossed the camera at them and Quinn caught it midair before it could hit Amelia. "I don't have the stomach for this anymore. I'd like to say I hope you'll be happy together, but we all know I'd be lying." She turned on her heel and started walking down the street. "Taa taa, darlings."

Amelia pulled against Quinn's hold.

"Let her go," he muttered.

"She's. . .she's *vile!* I can't believe that woman is Astrid's sister."

He dropped the camera on the ground and turned her back into his arms, his hands sweeping down her back. "You know her?"

"Astrid? She sells coffee in James's building. And he's crazy about her. But he's had years to go against his family and marry her. Now that he's the Earl of Est-ingwood, he could do whatever he wants. But he won't."

"Why?"

"Because she's a commoner," Amelia said simply. "She's divorced. She has a child. Take your pick."

"I thought that stuff didn't matter anymore."

"It matters to the Bannings. And above all things, James is loyal to his family."

He pressed his lips against her temple. "I don't want to talk about James."

"Neither do I." From the corner of her eye, though, she kept watch of Ophelia, long enough to see the woman climb into an SUV and roar off down the street in the opposite direction.

Quinn suddenly pushed her away from him. "Where were we?"

Her throat tightened. "I don't know," she whispered.

"I do." Holding her hands, he abruptly went down on one knee, right there in the middle of the street. "I think this is the way it's supposed to go. Never did it before."

She inhaled sharply. "Quinn—"

"My heart is yours, Amelia Fortune Chesterfield. It has been from the second you agreed to a dance with a simple cowboy."

Tears flooded her eyes. "So is mine. Yours, I mean. My heart." She laughed brokenly. "I'm making a mish-mash. And there's nothing simple about you."

"Will you marry me?"

She nodded and pulled on his hands. "Yes. I don't want you on your knees, I just want you by my side."

He rose and caught her close. "Preacher or a JP?"

She dragged his head to hers. "As long as it's soon, I don't care," she said thickly, and pressed her mouth to his. Joy was bubbling through her, making her feel dizzy with it. "Take me home?"

He cradled her tightly, lifting her right off her feet. "Kissing me like that is how getting you pregnant started off," he warned. And then he laughed a little and swore. "I can't. I don't have my truck. I rode here with Jess."

She groaned. "I want to be alone with you." She sank her fingers through his hair, reveling in the realization that she *could*. "I don't care how shameless that sounds. I need to be alone with you."

"You're killing me," he said gruffly, and kissed her so softly, so sweetly, that she would have fallen in love with him all over again if she hadn't already done so.

Then he gently set her back on her feet. Kissed her forehead. Her cheeks. "We'll go back and borrow some keys from someone."

"And then you'll take me home?"

He lifted her hand and kissed her fingers. "And then I'll take you home." They started back toward the Cantina, but Amelia suddenly ducked under his arm and ran back to retrieve Ophelia's camera.

"What do you want that thing for?"

She pulled his arm over her shoulder once more and fiddled with the camera as they continued walking back to the Cantina. "There's got to be a memory card in here somewhere." She held up the camera, squinting in the light from the strands hanging in the trees. "Ah." She spotted the storage compartment and freed the tiny square inside before handing the camera to Quinn. "Don't toss that aside either," she warned. "There might be internal memory or something that will need to be erased."

"Ophelia's gone." He brushed his hand down her hair. "Nobody else is going to care about that thing."

"Probably," she agreed, "But I'm not taking any chances." She went over to one of the umbrella-covered tables and reached for one of the candles burning inside short jars. "Mind if I borrow this for a moment?" she asked the people sitting there, and when there were no objections, carried it back to him.

Holding the jar between them, she dropped the memory disk onto the flame. "No more Ophelia Malone," she murmured, watching the thing begin to sizzle and melt, and feeling like the last load was lifting from her shoulders.

When the memory card was no longer recognizable as anything but a misshapen blob of plastic, she blew out the candle and carefully plucked it out of the wax.

Then she dropped it on the road and ground it fervently beneath her heel.

Quinn lifted the candle out of her hand and set it back on the table. "Remind me never to make you really mad," he said when she finally stopped grinding.

"I know how to fox hunt, too," she told him, looping her arm through his. She couldn't seem to get the smile off her face, but then she couldn't imagine a reason why she needed to.

Quinn Drummond loved her.

What she'd feared was only a dream was real. And she was going to treasure that for the rest of their days.

"Fox hunt," he repeated warily. But he was smiling, too, and he absently hooked the camera strap over his shoulder.

"My father taught us." She looked up at the balcony above the umbrellas and saw her mother there, talking with Orlando Mendoza and looking unusually animated. "Once upon a time my father was a pilot," she murmured, nodding toward the balcony. "The Royal Air Force."

Quinn pulled her close against his side once more, as if he couldn't stand even a few inches separating them. He tilted his head looking upward, his gaze sharpening slightly. "They look—"

"Cozy," Amelia finished.

"Interesting." He steered her toward the entrance of the Cantina that was no less crowded than it had been earlier. "Maybe Horseback Hollow will end up appealing to more of the Fortune Chesterfields."

As much as the idea delighted her, she was presently more interested in Quinn. "You promised something about keys?"

"Yes, ma'am," Quinn said softly and kissed her right there in front of the Hollows Cantina for all the world to see. Then he tugged her after him through the crowds. Jess and Mac were sitting all cozied up together at their small table, clearly unworried whether he ever returned or not. The stairs were still crowded and he exhaled impatiently. But Amelia dragged him through the swinging doors to the kitchen where there was another staircase.

Not grand. Not the center of attention. But entirely welcome. At the top, he threaded his way around the tables there.

Lady Josephine was sitting once more next to Jeanne Marie and Deke and her smile deepened when she saw them. "Have you figured out where your fortune is, then, Quinn?"

"Yes, ma'am," he said and lifted his hand linked with

Amelia's. "I surely have." His eyes met Amelia's. "Love's the fortune."

Her smile trembled and she leaned into him. "Keys," she whispered.

He threw back his head and laughed. "Keys." He spotted Liam. "Lend me your truck for the night and I'll *consider* selling Rocky."

Liam reached into his pocket and tossed the keys over several heads. Quinn caught them handily.

Amelia giggled, squeezing his hand.

And they raced for the stairs.

Epilogue

Quinn parked his truck near the tree house tree and went around to open Amelia's door. "Come on."

She tilted her head up toward his, a smile on her face below the bandana he'd tied around her eyes before they'd left the ranch house.

It had been a week since the Cantina's grand opening. A week during which they'd barely left one another's side. A week in which it was finally sinking in that Amelia was his.

She loved him. She wasn't going anywhere. She was filling the empty parts of him, and together they'd fill the empty rooms of their home.

"What are we doing?" Her voice was full of laughter.

"You'll see." He took her hands and helped her out of the truck.

"Not exactly." Her lips tilted. "Since you've blindfolded me." She turned her head from side to side as he drew her closer to the tree, obviously trying to get a sense of where they were. "Do I hear the creek?"

He moved behind her and slid his hands around her waist and kissed her neck below her ear, right where he knew it would make her shiver. "Good instincts."

She sighed a little, shimmied a little with that shiver, and covered his hands with hers, pressing them against her belly. She rubbed her head against his chest. "On occasion. I picked you, didn't I?"

"That you did." He kissed her earlobe. "Okay, you can look."

She tugged the bandanna off her head.

"I knew it," she said, laughing in her triumph. She peered up into the tree branches. "You've finished the floor! When did you have time to do that?"

He'd finished a lot more than that. "When you're lazing around in bed, snoring."

"I don't snore."

"You do." He kissed her nose. "Daintily. Like the lady that you are."

She rolled her eyes. "Oh, that makes it all right then."

He laughed softly. "It's safe for us to go up."

Her dark eyes roved over his face while a smile played around her soft lips. "*Us?* As in now you're going to let me climb a tree?"

His hands slid down her hips. "Only because I'm here with you. So do you want to go up or not?"

Her eyes sparkled. "What do you think?" She quickly yanked off the sandals she'd been wearing and tossed them onto the grass, then set her bare toes on the first foothold and deftly began climbing.

"Just go slow, okay? Be careful."

She looked over her shoulder at him, grinning and looking more like a teenaged girl than a pregnant woman. "Fine warning from the man who puts temptation in my path."

She continued up with Quinn standing below her, and between his distraction over the view of her bare legs beneath her summery pink dress as she went, even he had to admit that she seemed to know exactly what she was doing. "How often did you say you used to climb trees?"

She laughed. She'd reached the base of the tree house and pushed open the door in the floor. "Every day that I could get away with it." In seconds, she'd clambered through the hatch, and then there was only silence.

He imagined her up there, seeing the preparations he'd made early that morning while she'd been sleeping in his bed.

Their bed.

A moment later, she leaned over the high side boards that formed the walls of the tree house, her long hair hanging down past her shoulders. Her youthful grin was gone, replaced by a soft expression. "Are you going to stand around down there, or join me?"

He kicked off his own shoes and climbed up.

It didn't take him any longer than it had her, but in that brief time she'd still managed to slip out of her dress, and was laying on the thick blankets he'd spread out on one side of the structure.

He let out a breath.

She propped her head on her hand and smiled slightly, holding one of the daisies he'd stuck in a jar to her nose. She was wearing sheer panties and a bra the same pale blue color as the Texas sky. "This *is* what you had in mind, isn't it?"

He crawled through the door and dropped it back in place. "Yeah." He shucked his own clothes, pitching them in the corner.

Her lashes swept down and pink color touched her cheeks. "I'm wondering if Peter Pan ever got up to such mischief."

He knelt down beside her, and she rolled onto her back, her hair pooling out around her head. "Peter Pan was a boy," he murmured, sliding one strap off her shoulder and kissing the creamy skin there.

She ran her thigh against his as she bent her knee and dropped the flower in favor of closing her hand boldly around him. "And you're *no* boy."

He exhaled on a rough laugh and caught her hand in his, pulling it away. "Not so fast, Lady Fortune Chesterfield." He stretched out next to her and slid off the other bra strap, then unsnapped the tiny silver clasp between her breasts holding it together. "I have plans for you."

"That'll be Mrs. Drummond—" her voice hitched when he caught one of those rosy crests between his lips "—to you."

He smiled against her warm flesh. Already he could sense small changes in her body because of the baby inside her. Her breasts were fuller. Her nipples a deeper pink. "Soon as you finally say whether you want a minister or a justice of the peace, that's who you'll be." He kissed his way down her flat belly, anchoring her hips gently when she shivered and twisted against him.

"Minister," she whispered. Her fingers slid through his hair, clutching. "And soon."

He nuzzled his way beneath the sexy little panties that matched the bra. "Impatient to make this all legal?"

"Yes." She suddenly twisted, reversing their positions

and pinned him on the blankets. "And I want to say yes before I'm big as a house. But I want my brothers and sister here, too. And you'll need a suit since you lost your jacket at the Cantina the other night." She kicked off her panties and sank down on him, letting out a shuddering moan.

He clamped his hands over her hips. "You're not always gonna get your way like this, princess." He sucked in a sharp breath as she rocked her hips against him. "I'm only indulging this need for constant speed you've got 'cause—"

"You love me." She leaned over, rubbing her tight nipples against his chest, and kissed him.

"—you're pregnant and at the mercy of your hormones," he finished.

Then, wrapping his arm around her waist, he flipped her onto her back. Loving the color in her cheeks and the way her eyes went an even darker brown, soft as down and feeling like home.

"And because I love you," he said the words quietly. They were coming easier, but even when he didn't say them he wanted her to know he would never stop feeling them.

Her eyes turned shiny and wet. She laid her palm along his jaw and brushed her thumb over his lip. "If I'm a princess, you know that makes you my prince."

"I don't care what you call me, Amelia—" he sank into her "—as long as it means *husband*."

She gasped, and twined her legs around his hips, arching against him. "This…tree house is off-limits the second our son—"

"Daughter—"

"—hits puberty," she managed breathlessly.

He laughed and thumbed away the tears leaking from her big brown eyes. "Damn straight it is," he agreed.

And then he kissed her and together, they flew.

* * * * *

COMING NEXT MONTH FROM

H HARLEQUIN®

SPECIAL EDITION

Available June 19, 2014

#2341 MILLION-DOLLAR MAVERICK
Montana Mavericks: 20 Years in the Saddle! • by Christine Rimmer
Cowboy Nate Crawford epitomizes the phrase "new money." He secretly just won millions in the lottery, and he can't wait to cash out and leave Rust Creek Falls. But then Nate meets gorgeous nurse Callie Kennedy, who doesn't give a flying Stetson about money, and all he's ever dreamed of might be in the home he wants to leave behind....

#2342 DATING FOR TWO
Matchmaking Mamas • by Marie Ferrarella
Erin O'Brien is too busy bringing her toy company to new heights to play house with just any man. But speaking at a local Career Day might lead to a whole new job—mommy! When she meets hunky lawyer Steve Kendall and his son, Erin can't help but fall for the adorable twosome. Will Erin be the missing piece in their family puzzle?

#2343 THE BACHELOR'S BRIGHTON VALLEY BRIDE
Return to Brighton Valley • by Judy Duarte
Clayton Jenkins is going undercover...in his own business. The tech whiz wants to find out why his flagship store is failing, so he disguises himself as an employee and gets to work. But even a genius can't program every step of his life—like falling for single mom Megan Adams and her young children! What's a billionaire to do?

#2344 READY, SET, I DO!
Rx for Love • by Cindy Kirk
Workaholic Winn Ferris receives the surprise of his life when he gets custody of an eight-year-old boy. He enlists neighbor Hailey Randall to help him with the child, but Winn can't help but marvel at the bubbly speech therapist. She might just be the one to lift the businessman's nose from the grindstone to gaze into her beautiful baby blues—and fall in love....

#2345 A BRIDE BY SUMMER
Round-the-Clock Brides • by Sandra Steffen
Apple orchard owner Reed Sullivan is frantic with worry when a baby appears on his doorstep. Did his one-night stand from a year ago yield a (too) fruitful crop? So Reid's blindsided when a radiant redhead rescues him from a car accident. Ruby O'Toole has sworn off men, but the quirky bar owner might have it bad for the man she saved—and his insta-family!

#2346 A DOCTOR FOR KEEPS
by Lynne Marshall
Desdemona "Desi" Rask shows up on her grandmother's doorstep to learn about her family in the town of Heartlandia. But Fate throws a wrench in her plans when she meets Dr. Kent Larson and his adorable son. As Desi discovers more about her relatives, she wonders: Can she have a future with Kent, or will her past keep them apart forever?

YOU CAN FIND MORE INFORMATION ON UPCOMING HARLEQUIN® TITLES, FREE EXCERPTS AND MORE AT WWW.HARLEQUIN.COM.

HSECNM0614

REQUEST YOUR FREE BOOKS!

2 FREE NOVELS PLUS 2 FREE GIFTS!

ⓗ HARLEQUIN®

SPECIAL EDITION

Life, Love & Family

YES! Please send me 2 FREE Harlequin® Special Edition novels and my 2 FREE gifts (gifts are worth about $10). After receiving them, if I don't wish to receive any more books, I can return the shipping statement marked "cancel." If I don't cancel, I will receive 6 brand-new novels every month and be billed just $4.74 per book in the U.S. or $5.24 per book in Canada. That's a savings of at least 14% off the cover price! It's quite a bargain! Shipping and handling is just 50¢ per book in the U.S. and 75¢ per book in Canada.* I understand that accepting the 2 free books and gifts places me under no obligation to buy anything. I can always return a shipment and cancel at any time. Even if I never buy another book, the two free books and gifts are mine to keep forever.

235/335 HDN F45Y

Name _____ (PLEASE PRINT)

Address _____ Apt. #

City _____ State/Prov. _____ Zip/Postal Code

Signature (if under 18, a parent or guardian must sign)

Mail to the Harlequin® Reader Service:
IN U.S.A.: P.O. Box 1867, Buffalo, NY 14240-1867
IN CANADA: P.O. Box 609, Fort Erie, Ontario L2A 5X3

Want to try two free books from another line?
Call 1-800-873-8635 or visit www.ReaderService.com.

* Terms and prices subject to change without notice. Prices do not include applicable taxes. Sales tax applicable in N.Y. Canadian residents will be charged applicable taxes. Offer not valid in Quebec. This offer is limited to one order per household. Not valid for current subscribers to Harlequin Special Edition books. All orders subject to credit approval. Credit or debit balances in a customer's account(s) may be offset by any other outstanding balance owed by or to the customer. Please allow 4 to 6 weeks for delivery. Offer available while quantities last.

Your Privacy—The Harlequin® Reader Service is committed to protecting your privacy. Our Privacy Policy is available online at www.ReaderService.com or upon request from the Harlequin Reader Service.

We make a portion of our mailing list available to reputable third parties that offer products we believe may interest you. If you prefer that we not exchange your name with third parties, or if you wish to clarify or modify your communication preferences, please visit us at www.ReaderService.com/consumerchoice or write to us at Harlequin Reader Service Preference Service, P.O. Box 9062, Buffalo, NY 14269. Include your complete name and address.

HSE13R

SPECIAL EXCERPT FROM

◆ **H** HARLEQUIN®

™

SPECIAL EDITION

Enjoy this sneak preview of
DATING FOR TWO
by USA TODAY *bestselling author Marie Ferrarella!*

***

"Well, you'll be keeping your word to them—I'll be the one doing the cooking."

One of the things he'd picked up on during his brief venture into the dating realm was that most professional women had no time—or desire—to learn how to cook. He'd just naturally assumed that Erin was like the rest in that respect.

"Didn't you say that you were too busy trying to catch up on everything you'd missed out on doing because you were in the hospital?"

"Yes, and cooking was one of those things." She laughed. "A creative person has to have more than one outlet in order to feel fulfilled and on top of their game. Me, I come up with some of my best ideas cooking. Cooking relaxes me," she explained.

"Funny, it has just the opposite effect on me," he said.

"Your strengths obviously lie in other directions," she countered.

Steve had to admit he appreciated the way she tried to spare his ego.

He watched Erin as she practically whirled through his kitchen, getting unlikely ingredients out of his pantry and his cupboard. She assembled everything on the counter within easy reach, then really got busy as she began making dinner.

He had never been one who enjoyed being kept in the dark. "If you don't mind my asking, exactly what do you plan on making?"

"A frittata," she said cheerfully. Combining a total of eight eggs in a large bowl, she tossed in a dash of salt and pepper before going on to add two packages of the frozen mixed vegetables. She would have preferred to use fresh vegetables, but beggars couldn't afford to be choosers.

"A what?"

In another pan, she'd quickly diced up some of the ham she'd found as well as a few slices of cheddar cheese from the same lower bin drawer in the refrigerator.

She was about to repeat the word, then realized that it wasn't that Steve hadn't heard her—the problem was that he didn't know what she was referring to.

Opening the pantry again, she searched for a container of herbs or spices. There were none. She pushed on anyway, adding everything into the bowl with the eggs.

"Just think of it as an upgraded omelet. You have ham and bread," she said, pleased.

"That's because I also know how to make a sandwich without setting off the smoke alarm," he told her.

"There is hope for you yet," she declared with a laugh.

Watching her move around his kitchen as if she belonged there, he was beginning to think the same thing himself—but for a very different reason.

***

Don't miss DATING FOR TWO,
coming July 2014 from Harlequin® Special Edition.

⬦ HARLEQUIN®

SPECIAL EDITION

Life, Love and Family

20 Years in the Saddle!

Celebrate 20 years of *The Montana Mavericks*
this July with

MILLION-DOLLAR MAVERICK

from *USA TODAY* bestselling author

Christine Rimmer

Cowboy Nate Crawford epitomizes the phrase *new money*. He secretly just won millions in the lottery, and he can't wait to cash out and leave Rust Creek Falls. But then Nate meets gorgeous nurse Callie Kennedy, who doesn't give a flying Stetson about money, and all he's ever dreamed of might be in the home he wants to leave behind....

Available wherever books and ebooks are sold!

HSE65823